# Deluge:

# Stories of
# Survival &
# Tragedy in the
# Great Flood

## Biblical Legends Anthology
## Series

Jo,
thanks for being an
awesome reader

Allen

**Edited by Allen Taylor**
Published By Garden Gnome Publications

**Cover art by Alexandre Rito**

# Table of Contents

ALPHA ................................................................................. 1

FLASH FICTIONS ................................................................ 4

   1 AS BIG AS ALL THE WORLD ...................................... 5

   2 GUIDANCE IN THE CLOUDS ...................................... 7

   3 DREAMS OF THE MOON ........................................... 10

   4 PLANET TERRUS ....................................................... 13

   5 TEN LONELY RAIN GODS ......................................... 15

   6 AN IRONCLAD FATE OF HER OWN DESIGN ........... 18

   7 PROBLEM POINTS .................................................... 20

   8 WAVES AS A BOND WITH GOD ............................... 23

   9 S' DAY ........................................................................ 25

IOTA .................................................................................. 29

   10 AQUALUNG ............................................................ 30

SHORT STORIES ............................................................... 32

   11 FIELDS OF THE NEPHILIM ................................... 33

   12 DREAMERS OF THE DELUGE ................................ 37

   13 THE IMMERSION OF THE INCORPOREUM .......... 43

   14 REMNANTS OF THE FLOOD ................................. 56

   15 SURVEYING SAVIORS ........................................... 73

   16 THE SHARPTOOTH ................................................ 80

OMEGA .............................................................................. 90

   17 ANGELBLOOD ....................................................... 91

BIOS .................................................................................. 128

ABOUT THE EDITOR ...................................................... 131

This anthology is dedicated to anyone and everyone who has ever looked, felt, tasted, or smelled like a garden gnome and their relatives, owners, assigns, foot props, and nearby tree stumps.

# ALPHA

## Allen Taylor

When I first conceptualized the Biblical Legends Anthology Series (BLAS), I had no idea how the anthologies would be received. I also had no idea what quality of writing I would see or the nature of the content. I'm quite pleased.

*Garden of Eden* came first. The smallest of the three, it set the expectations for the others to follow. Writers seemed to understand what I was aiming at. I followed it with *Sulfurings: Tales from Sodom & Gomorrah*, which took a different, more apocalyptic, turn. While out of order from the biblical timeline, the second and third (*Deluge: Stories of Survival & Tragedy in the Great Flood*) books in the series attracted a grittier, darker form of literature. Again, the writers did not disappoint.

Selling at physical events has allowed me to assess reader reactions in a way that can't be done online. Generally, I see three types of reactions:

1. Enthusiastic acceptance for a unique idea;

2. Gross rejection, or absolute shock;

3. Or an assumption that, because they're based on Bible stories, they are "Christian" in nature.

Naturally, I'm thankful for the first type of reader, and the second type isn't my audience. The third type of reader, however, falls into two categories. The first category is the devout Christian expecting the stories to be "family-friendly" or hail from a Christian point of view. The other category is the non-Christian who assumes the same.

While some of the stories are written by authors approaching the subject matter from an orthodox Christian perspective, not all the stories fall in that line. The truth is, I didn't ask writers about their backgrounds. It didn't occur to me to do so because I was simply looking for good stories with a speculative twist on the biblical narratives. We weren't reinventing theology. We were reimagining literature.

Readers may find some of the details in certain stories inaccurate, or they may disagree with a writer's interpretation of the events. Both are fair assessments. On the other hand, readers may find some interesting explorations of sin, redemption, righteousness, God's wrath, and other biblical themes. These themes may be explored even as events stray from the biblical storyline. In other cases, the themes are explored satirically.

When asking for submissions, I made two stipulations. First, I wanted stories set during the biblical Great Flood or that explored the flood theme in a new and different way. I also asked writers not to include biblical characters in their stories. Fortunately, a few of the authors broke that rule.

Some stories in *Deluge* may present elements that are offensive to some readers. Such is the nature of literature. No apologies warranted or granted.

Changes made to this second edition begin and end with author bios. The stories are the same. I requested that authors update their bios for the second printing. Most added publishing credits or changed their credits to more recent ones. Some didn't respond at all. One author took the liberty of announcing his transgender status. I didn't expect that. Inclusion of that author's story may invite controversy of its own, for reasons that have nothing to do with literature or the purpose of these anthologies. I didn't think it would be fair to ask him to edit his bio (since I didn't ask anyone else to edit theirs), nor would it be fair to pull his story based on some moral sensibility, whether mine or someone else's. That may have some readers question my judgment or accusing me of "endorsing" transgenderism. That author's story stands on its own merit, and his own lifestyle choices are subject to God's judgment (as are mine and everyone else's).

In short, I'm an editor and publisher, not the moral police and certainly not the thought police. Nevertheless, I'm delighted that writers and readers alike may be driven to the Bible to read the text where the original stories can be found, and I hope this anthology honor the original story in some way even if individual literary creations stray far afield.

And now, without further ado, I present *Deluge: Stories of Survival & Tragedy in the Great Flood.*

# FLASH FICTIONS

# 1 AS BIG AS ALL THE WORLD

## John Vicary

The Arctic sun dawned under a canopy of clouds in the north. Anuniaq and Karpok paid the dim orb no heed; they had a job to finish regardless of the light or lack thereof. The remnants of snow from a full night away must be cleared. The men worked in wordless communion to bare the frozen face of the life-sustaining sea.

When the holes were cut into the thick ice and the poles laid with bait, the men sat together in stillness and watched the snow fall in unabating drifts from the Great Above.

"It's a long spell of *kanevvluk* this season," Anuniaq said at last.

Karpok grunted.

"I heard old Uglu speaking about it last night at the Gathering. He said we might hit forty days and forty nights since the first *qanuk* fell. Isn't that something?" Anuniaq asked.

Karpok shrugged. His name meant "hungry", and he was rarely interested in anything beyond the subject of his namesake. He reached over and inspected the pole, then dropped his mittened hand again.

Anuniaq didn't mind talking to himself; the silence of the open plain could drive a man crazy. "Well, last year it was thirty-seven days, and the year before that it was thirty-nine. Old Uglu thinks that we'll hit the record. If it snows one more night, we'll make it. Huh."

The line twitched and Karpok pulled a wriggling whitefish from the frigid water. The lines on his weathered face deepened with the first smile of the morning. He held up his catch in triumph before rethreading the line.

After another hour and two more fish, Anuniaq began talking again. "Can you imagine if this wasn't *kanevvluk*?"

"What?" The absurdity of the question startled Karpok into speech. "What else would Qailertetang send to us?"

"Think of the southern tribes. They might be having rain," Anuniaq said. In truth, he'd wondered that for some time. He'd had a dream once of that very thing, and in his spare moments he'd embroidered it more vividly with each imagining. How did the men of the south cope?

Karpok scoffed. "There are no southern tribes."

"But think of it." Now Anuniaq's fancy had taken flight. "It would rain and rain and they would have to build a kayak to stay afloat. I wonder how they would keep the oil dry? What would happen to the caribou?"

Karpok laughed. "It would need to be a kayak as big as all the world. I'm glad I live in the north. Even the *muruaneq* ... chk!" He made a sound through his teeth. "We can clear it away, just like that. Be glad there is no one in the world to drown in the waters. Aakuluujjusi is good to give us our home here. We are patient with whitefish until summer. We shall grow fat on walrus and elk again. Your brain has caught a fever with eating only winter hare, I think."

Anuniaq laughed. "No, my friend. I was just wondering of other places."

"Bah!" Karpok made a face. "Who cares of other places? There is no place but here."

As the line twitched, Anuniaq pulled in a trout. Snow melted on the silvered scales of the dying fish, and Anuniaq sent a prayer of thanks to Agloolik for their hunt.

"Come." Karpok stood and hefted his catch onto his shoulder. "We shall go home and feed our village. You will forget your strange ideas when you have a bellyful of fish. Rain to cover the world and a kayak to float the tribes of the south? Even Agloolik in his mischief would not be so evil. Bah."

Anuniaq looked into the round hole of open water beneath his feet for a long moment before turning away. He was careful to place his mukluks in the steps laid out by his friend and followed the path all the way home.

# 2 GUIDANCE IN THE CLOUDS

## JD DeHart

NOA72 twirled down the narrow hallway of space deck fourteen. His memory deck played the image of the ghostly figure, like Hamlet's father, appearing on the outer deck a few months prior. It had been a rainless afternoon after decades of drought. The world was as cracked and dry as a desert hobo's upper lip.

"#endoftheworld," the ghostly figure reported. "#buttloadofwater."

"#got2bejokin," replied NOA72, to which the ghostly figure just shook his ethereal head. "#whodis?"

"#therealgodhead."

"#thoughtyouweredead."

"#godsnotdead."

With that, the astral figure disappeared, and bits of the mission began to fall into place. There was some vague direction, as if there was a pipeline to prophecy and the bot had just accessed it.

Since that brief conversation, NOA72 had started the project: A spaceship that would hold DNA specimens of all the creatures on his planet. The plan, as he understood it, was to re-colonize a different world, perhaps spiraling into a different universe. There was the vague feeling that this had

7

all happened before, maybe even multiple times.

The lovely KTRA26, a much younger iteration of android, cooed to NOA72, "#areumental?"

"#keepinitreal, #gottogetbusy," replied the other.

"#seriously, #comeoutandplay, #blushingafternoon."

"#onamissionfromgod."

KTRA26 left sadly. She knew that this android, this NOA iteration, was slightly crazy for building this ship and collecting all the scraps of fauna. She had noticed him, just a few days ago, trying to sneak up on a quick lizard, a scalpel in his grip.

Still, there was something vaguely attractive about him. KTRA26 had a crush on the handsome android, and even though he was mental, she wanted to be on the ship with him. She wondered briefly if he was one of those Bible-thumping bots, refusing to think for himself, always going back to the same proof-texts. He did not seem that way.

NOA72 watched her form fade into the distance. There were only three specimens left to collect. He would find them easily the next day, he calculated, and already had a heat signature on two of them.

By an hour later, the sky had begun to blacken. KTRA26 was piling one stone on top of another, a popular pastime on the inhospitable planet, when she clicked and whirred at the sky. She immediately thought of the ship, detecting a hint of moisture in the air.

NOA72 was placing the last of the DNA strands in place and just about to pull the ship's hatch shut for good when he heard: "#doomsday, #istherestillroomintheinn?" Rain was beginning to pound down now.

"#chopchop," he replied.

Unfortunately, the precipitation had made the outside of the craft unusually slippery.

"#whatdoIdo? #madeofmetal," KTRA26 said.

"#holdontosomething."

Little by little, the female android made it up the sleek surface and down the hatch, the world closing out. The sound of rain made great thumps and

NOA72 hit the ignition, throwing the ship into movement as great waves came cascading in, bursting as if the sky had been holding its mouth shut.

"#fortydaysandfortynights," said NOA72.

"#travelgames," KTRA26 replied, and the two of them entwined their sensors and made for the living room deck.

# 3 DREAMS OF THE MOON

## Lorina Stephens

In the darkness that follows disaster, he hears the river. It sounds like the rush of beating wings, pulling the host of Elohim into conflict, and for some, into escape. He is unsure who has followed, or who has betrayed them. Michael? Raphael? Who among the Iyrin hadn't wanted to teach those beautiful mortals?

He gropes the air before him, feels nothing, moves toward the sound of the river, finds a rough texture under his fingers—bark, it's still here—and hands himself down to sit beneath the tree. There is pain. This is something new to him, a sinister sensation in the darkness, he who has lived his life in the chiaroscuro of light. Sariel, whose name was written on shields, whose name was an invocation of death from the Third Tower and he, the Bringer of Death. The Captain Sariel, now blind, unable to fly, waiting here at the edge of the river and the fourth paradise, for what? He's unsure and wishing for death.

He thinks he might laugh for the absurdity of it. It's too much to think about. Too much has happened. He eases further down in darkness to fragrant myrtle, dew on his arm, pain in one wing where he knows it's broken and pain where his eyes once saw the phases of the moon. He lets the darkness and the rush of the river become an anodyne for his senses.

He listens to the river. There is only one way to cross it now. Impossible to fly with this broken wing and sightless eyes.

"Sariel." He hears and stirs, unsure if he's imagining this through the miasma of his pain. He wishes he could see. He wishes he could know the minds of others as he once had.

"Shamsiel?" he asks. His voice sounds hoarse to him. It is a rattle in the darkness.

"No," the voice answers. "Shamsiel is fallen."

Fallen. Then Eden has fallen, for Shamsiel and that host were to defend Eden. All is lost. "Are they safe? The Chosen, the Nephilim?" Is she safe? Is the child?

"Yes. We're all safe."

And doomed to exist on Mount Hermon in the Cave of Treasures, they and their Nephilim. "And the other Iyrin with us?"

"All fallen. You are the last."

With that realization, Sariel weeps. So much has been lost. The City of Light is no longer theirs, nor is the world they'd hoped to make with The Chosen, and the children they would rear together.

He feels lips on his eyes, and hears the voice of his rescuer, sibilant in the darkness. There are words to comfort and to soothe, and Sariel sinks into the other's arms, letting grief wash over him. It is the woman he's taken as mate he now knows. Her hands touch his face and the wounds of his eyes. He can feel her trembling, or is that him?

"I know, I know," she says, and there is rocking, something the Iyrin learned from mortal humans, an expression of a need for comfort. "Only a little more pain now. And it will all be done."

A little more pain explodes into suffocating terror. He screams. And then again as the terror repeats. The darkness is filled with the sound and smell of it. With one hand, he reaches out toward her, finds an arm, a hand. The hilt of his own fiery sword has been used to sever wings, and now he is truly afraid because her voice still croons, and she still rocks him.

"Why?" he manages to gasp.

"To bind you. To disguise you against the hunt that has come. All the others have been cast forever into darkness, and I would have you live with me. Be mortal. Die."

Sariel, the Prince of Death, to die himself.

He sinks into oblivion, unable to bear the pain. When again he rises, he is still in darkness, still rocking, only now there is music, a voice in melancholy song. In another moment of panic, he realizes he's on a boat.

He calls out. He hears her voice.

"You're awake," she says.

"Where are you taking me?" He knows, but there is always hope. He's learned this from his sojourn in Eden.

"To the others."

"And so, we are all outcasts?"

"All. And bound."

"Is this death?"

"Very like, I suppose."

She dissembles, he knows. "How?" He can hear no answer, and bound in darkness he cannot see any gesture that might illuminate the question. It is then when he confronts the fact of mortality, and what it was to be Iyrin. He has heard for the dead there is cessation of pain. It is what he believed, being the Prince of Death. So many lives he has transmuted with the power of his sword. But, for the Iyrin, there would be everlasting knowledge of what they've lost and will never again see, or know, cast out as others are. She has given him a choice, now, to live or to die.

And so, Sariel, father of one of the Nephilim, mate of a human woman, once favored among the Iyrin, master of the phases of the moon, does what he is doomed to do: he seizes that fiery sword, pushes himself out of the boat, and smites himself. He sinks down into the frigid water, dreaming of beauty. Dreaming of death.

# 4 PLANET TERRUS

## Tom Mollica

Watching the hologram, Cacho Zahn saw a being emerge from a dwelling. "The specimen is outside," Cacho said to the number one pilot, the only other person in the ship's control room. He also observed the same happenings below on a hologram that was four times the size of Cacho's. The mappers had designated this planet with the title of Terrus.

"Yes," Number One answered. A number one pilot's verbal communications with the lower-level working party was minimal. Cacho and Number One watched in silence for a time until Number One spoke again. "It is time for us to act." He pointed his long and thin gray finger towards the panel in front of him.

In the center of the control room, a hologram appeared showing the transport room of the ship. There, two knowledge seekers dressed in their usual white tunics stood next to a midsized vessel. The craft was not saucer-shaped like the space travel ships Cacho was accustomed to. It was rectangular and boxy. Its design was similar to the dwellings from the area below but longer with four levels.

"We are ready," Number One voiced to the knowledge seekers. "Are all the specimens stored?"

"Yes, Number One," A knowledge seeker answered, and motioned with a three-fingered gray hand to the ship. "Every specimen we deem beneficial to this world has been accumulated, and the DNA cells stored in their control units inside the vessel. They will be ready to be reborn when it is time."

"Launch arc," Number One said and pointed a finger towards the panel, which caused the knowledge seeker's hologram to vanish.

Cacho watched on his hologram as the vessel was launched from the solar sail saucer and hovered. It landed in plants next to the farmer's home and crushed them as the specimen watched. A female specimen and two under-developed smaller ones joined him. A side panel on the ship opened and a ramp extended downward.

Number One again pointed a finger to his control panel. In the sky above the family a large image appeared of a head that was a likeness of the aliens on the planet. The white-skinned head was too small in proportion to the body size, Cacho thought. Even though his race had much smaller bodies than the hominids, their heads were close to three times as large as the alien's. The beings' heads were oval-shaped. Cacho's was triangular with rounded corners. The alien portrayed in the sky image had a face that featured hair on the cheeks, and long brown hair. It was nothing like the smooth, hairless heads of Cacho's people.

The specimen below looked up as the head spoke in a booming, deep voice. "Noah, it is time."

Cacho and Number One watched the family return to the home, gather a few things, and step back out. The four entered the ship and the ramp slid back in, then the panel closed.

Number One spoke into the control panel. "Release the fountains of the great deep."

On the planet, water from rivers, lakes, and oceans began to overflow. Larger and darker stratocumulus clouds joined the stealth cloud surrounding Cacho's vessel just as thrusters ignited beneath the saucer and lifted it upward. The moment it was above the clouds, the skies let loose with a heavy downpour of driving rain.

Number One again spoke into his control panel, "Set course to return after forty days and forty nights."

# 5 TEN LONELY RAIN GODS

## David Macpherson

The first lonely rain god sits on her bed and sings, "Cry Me a River." She looks up and says, "That's a joke. Cry me a river. That's a lot of tears. I'm a rain god. I was crying and so it's funny because, ah, forget it." She sings the song from the beginning, but not knowing all the words, hums most of it.

The second lonely rain god writes words on a dry erase board with a squeaky marker. He writes: drought, deluge, downpour, arid, sprinkle, giraffe. He pauses. "I just like writing the word. *Giraffe.* You try it. *Giraffe.* It's fun on the fingers as it slides into letters. *Giraffe.* Now try *Deluge.* See. There is no fun in that word."

The third lonely rain god paces back and forth on the basketball court, mumbling to himself, "El Niño. El Niño. El Niño. Worst kind of false advertising I know. Little boy. Little boy. I created floods and storms and imminent destruction, and they call me the little boy. Put me in short pants, pat my head, and shove a chicklet in my mouth. El Niño. Good boy. Go down to the basement fridge and get daddy another beer. My father did that to me once. I blocked the drains in the basement sink and opened the taps. I got daddy his beer, and by the time they realized what I had done, the basement was flooded, and the house's structure was ruined. I'm nobody's El Niño."

The fourth and fifth lonely rain gods are in the rec room playing ping pong. Every volley echoes down the hall. They don't know what the score is. They don't know who is winning. "But I know who is losing," one of them says. "You can always notice the losers. Winners are tougher. Harder to see,"

15

the other one says. "Serve already. Stop making speeches." The serve hits the table like heat lightning. Eventually, the game is called on account of rain.

The sixth lonely rain god is working on a paint-by-numbers set. "Don't laugh," she says. "They're relaxing, and they're popular. Maybe even hip. I said, don't laugh. You're breaking my concentration." She furrows her brow and carefully fills in the #14 spot with light magenta. "But this one's defective. The box illustration shows Noah and the Ark and the two by two and all that propaganda, but that's not the picture I'm filling in. It's like a Mardi Gras parade or something with floats and beads raining down from balconies. I guess I can complain, but I'm too relaxed. Paint by numbers is relaxing."

The seventh lonely rain god—let's skip the seventh lonely rain god. It's for the best.

The eighth lonely rain god is sleeping. Or maybe he's pretending to be asleep. His ear buds are leaking out a meditation CD with the sounds of summer showers and crashing waves. Let's let him sleep or let him continue pretending.

The ninth lonely rain god strums undiscovered chords on her boyfriend's guitar. She is humming. I'm sorry, but the seventh lonely rain god is back and refuses to be passed over. I tried, but there she is in her bathrobe and mismatched fuzzy slippers. One foot is a teddy bear and the other is a porpoise. She is standing there giving that look she gives. The one that compels umbrellas to spontaneously open and slickers to tremble all through the building complex. She says, "Once entire nations worshipped me. They made bloody sacrifices to me. Sometimes I would deign to acknowledge their offerings with a humble shower. But now, they toss the runes of fronts and high-pressure systems. Al Roker is a false god. The Weather Channel is a heretical temple."

The ninth lonely rain god has left. I suppose she couldn't hang around any longer. But where she was is a piece of paper with some writing on it. It might be a poem. "The girl with the life preserver heart is floating in the deluge. Her love is the wave crashing like persistence. Her hope is a chant. She shouts adoration that cannot be heard. She wants to dry each other clean and blessed. They will release the livestock and live like Utnapishtim at the Mouth of the Rivers." That's what's written there. I guess some folks might call it a poem. I guess.

The tenth lonely rain god is pacing with the phone to his ear. They put him on hold and now he waits to speak to a supervisor. He's going to let

them have it. Going to let it go, open the floodgates. It will be wet and
But for now, he waits. And waits. And listens to the piped-in music for th
on hold: "Cry Me a River."

# 6 AN IRONCLAD FATE OF HER OWN DESIGN

## Sarah Vernetti

The rain had pummeled their home for days, the droplets hitting the marble patio with such force that they sprang back into the air only to fall again, making the torrential rain seem that much more impressive.

Margo knew what was coming. In her mind, she could see herself gasping for air, reaching skyward for dry land that did not exist.

It didn't cross her mind to tell her parents. After all, they already knew. Every member of their species could see these glimpses of the future. Surely, the scenario had already danced through their minds. Already they had watched their fourth and youngest daughter drown.

Margo pondered her next move. Although she could see the future, she had no way of knowing when the end would arrive. Could she alter her fate? Was the final result cast in bronze or precariously pieced together in gauze?

She turned away from one of the palace's many windows, from the image of her lungs filling with wrathful water and grabbed her satchel.

When she arrived at the general store, she was told that they were sold out of all wooden planks and tools. Apparently, those items, along with several barrels of flour, four pounds of salt, and ten bushels of vegetables, had been purchased by a previous customer.

"Noah," Margo thought to herself as she squinted at the store owner.

Despite her ability to see the future, Margo was a procrastinator. Once again, Noah had been one step ahead of her and the rest of her species.

She walked out of the store and made her way to the wash, which was already suffering from a flash flood. The rain was still pouring. Instead of fighting against the marble of her patio, here, the rain surrendered and was absorbed immediately into the ever-growing pool.

Without pausing to look back, without thinking again of the warm palace from which she had come, Margo walked toward the wash, stepped off the edge, and began to live the vision that had danced in her head for weeks.

If she couldn't float like Noah, then down to the depths she would travel. On her own time.

# 7 PROBLEM POINTS

## E.S. Wynn

When the flood came, Noah built a boat because God told him to.

But God didn't have to tell Doctor Lilith R. Thudmucker to build a boat. She'd already built something better. She'd built a time machine.

Her mission was simple. Centuries of research into biblical accounts of history had turned up certain *problem points,* as they were known: gaps glossed over in Genesis but explored or hinted at in other, older texts.

One such point was the Noah story, and it was Doctor Thudmucker who finally connected the dots across several sources in the summer of 2069. The revelation came suddenly and shockingly; while Noah had built a boat to save himself, his wife and his sons' wives, there were indications that someone had arrived from *some other time* to warn of the flood and stage an evacuation of some of the largest cities on the face of the antediluvian earth.

Someone who, from descriptions Lilith had read in a crumbling scroll that had spent centuries in the darkness of a dusty cave in Iraq, looked a lot like she did.

That was when the plan began to come together.

Years upon years of research passed. Components capable of manipulating time on a small scale were illegal and hard to find, but not impossible to acquire for the right price. The work was slow but precise, and as Doctor Thudmucker's time machine neared completion, she withdrew from society and civilization and spent every waking moment working on her plan of fine-tuning her machine.

When at last the day came to save the world from God's wrath and the in-breeding that would surely follow in the wake of his short-sighted need to spare only a single family of humans, Lilith took a day to rest and admire her creation. Despite its rough appearance, she decided it was good.

Doctor Thudmucker had spent years trying to decide which cities she would evacuate and in what order. Most were too sick with sin to consider saving, but in her view, a few were only slightly wicked. *And besides, any evil souls I might save by accident will only add spice to the mix,* she thought. *The world is full of jerks. They had to have come from somewhere.*

Deciding who would live and who would die made her feel like God, and in the end, she picked only seven cities to save. She wouldn't save everyone, only a smattering of interesting people who seemed good at heart. Fortunately, due to the nature of time (and the size of her time machine) she estimated that seven trips made to each city over the course of seven days would ensure an adequately sized gene pool to minimize in-breeding among the people who would become the ancestors of the postdiluvian human race.

Unfortunately, the first city she visited, a city which scant historical records had painted as a paragon of justice and righteousness, turned out to be a metropolis of ebon wood towers and slave markets called Jan'aloth.

There was no reasoning with the people of Jan'aloth. Like a choice slave, she was stripped and beaten almost the instant she set foot in the muddy streets, then chained and brought before the city's High Archon. Years spent studying the reconstructed tongue of the antediluvian world only earned her a slap and a smile, and the High Archon grinned as she wailed, trying to reason with him. What he understood of her babbling intrigued him, but not enough to spare her life. A knife across the throat ended her pleas, and then she was fed to the pigs, leaving only her time machine to attest to her appearance and her good intentions.

When it began to rain, just as Doctor Thudmucker had prophesied it would, the High Archon of Jan'aloth sent for seers and alchemists to study her time machine. As the waters rose, slaves of the High Archon beat the seers and alchemists harder to encourage them, but it wasn't until half of the city had sunk beneath the waves that anyone figured out how to work the vehicle. Lessons came quickly and secretively. Sternly attentive, the High Archon learned the art of flying the machine in a matter of hours, then killed everyone else who had seen it or knew of its existence. Secret orders went out to gather ten of his strongest soldiers, and as one, they raided the harems and slave markets of the dying city, stole two dozen fighting slaves, then returned to Doctor Thudmucker's time machine. Not even sparing a single glance for the city he had ruled with an iron fist for so long, the High Archon slammed the doors of the time machine and forced it forward, back to the century it had come from.

Panic ensued as thirty-five half-naked fighting men rippling with muscle shattered the front door of Doctor Thudmucker's home and descended upon the opulent, unprepared metropolis of New York. Blades of black steel flashed and felled hundreds of frail, pale humans caught in the streets, most of them before they could even look up from the screens printed in their meta-matter clothing. Videos of the assault went viral within minutes, but most people were too busy watching them or discussing what summer blockbuster the grainy, jumping clips might be preliminary trailers for. In the space of a few days, the High Archon of Jan'aloth was High Archon of New York, his army was burgeoning, and the slave markets he established in Pelham Bay Park rattled with the cracking of whips and the lamentations of men, women, and children.

But the luxuries of Thudmucker's time enchanted and snared him and soon he was utterly lost in a world of video games and VR porn. Some news stations hailed him as a hero and savior of the people. Dignitaries and diplomats carefully selected from among the people of the time kept the spin going and kept flattering images and promises on the air. When summer waned, the media campaign became a political campaign, and as the people and celebrities of the earth began parroting the slogan "Where is *our* High Archon?" it became clear that the world was about to be unified under a new world order over which the man who had been Jan'aloth's High Archon would reign unquestioned.

And so it was that God broke his covenant with man. With tired eyes, He reached into the mind of a wealthy entrepreneur in Silicon Valley named Noah and gave him very specific instructions on what to do with his money, his land, and the neo-hippie commune he called his family.

# 8 WAVES AS A BOND WITH GOD

## Carl Conrad

These were no ordinary waves; they yawned upward like a fifty- or sixty-foot mountain wall then crested into a curl with an ominous white froth that seemed as potentially deadly as an epileptic seizure before crashing with a force that obliterated everything in its path. It was relentless! The tide plundered its way into our domain with no observed limitations. Whatever was in its path was eliminated, crushed, and disemboweled.

I was more than two miles away on a high piece of ground that I always thought was impregnable. I loved the breathtaking sunsets, the steady but never oppressive breeze, the majesty of my solitude, and the spectacular beauty of my home. All that was imperiled by an angry wind. The turbulent sea was an unforgiving power that could change my life in an instant. Would everything I had worked for and cherished be taken away by one unrelenting and merciless storm?

The wind blew with a force that lashed streams of water across my face like the braids of a whip as I stood in front of my home, unmoving, defiant, but clearly only a twig in a forest of inestimable power. I felt the ceaseless, urgent press of water and gusting air as it attempted to blow everything that was not a part of the earth into dust and scrap. It pushed hard against me as I leaned into it with only my contempt and disgust to anchor me to this patch of quickly deteriorating ground.

Another wave surged over the treetops that I saw below me, pushing anything in its way ahead of it like an angry drunk sprawling across a tabletop. Homes, trees, boulders, boats, signs, cars—nothing was spared, and nothing resisted. The storm surge plowed through the countryside like the blade of a monstrous bulldozer. I saw a store lifted from its location. It pirouetted in the swiftly flowing onrush of water, then smashed against a village school that crumbled them both as if they were made of straw.

Homes, businesses, city infrastructure were all destroyed without conscience or exception. Would I lose all my possessions, too? Why? Was there a reason? What power could be so absolute and cruel to crush achievement, expunge effort, liquidate hope without regret or retribution? Was there someone guiding this pillage? Was this part of a divine plan? How could it be? Unless ...

I struggled to grasp insight. As suddenly as I thought of losing it all, it flashed through my mind that maybe it wasn't the loss of these things but the coveting of them that was so unbearable. Perhaps it was a bond that must be broken to allow something greater to emerge. It was not the possession of these things that was important but the ability to leave them behind that proved my independence and strengthened my bond with God.

I turned my back and knelt as I let it all go. Then I felt a release that truly changed my life.

# 9 S' DAY

## Kayleigh Edwards

Picture, if you will, a little sod. Everyone knows one; some of you might even have one. Hell, I bet a couple of you were right little sods yourselves. Now, imagine that you are the parent of said little sod, and he's playing up. He's been noisy in the supermarket; he's thrown his toy on the floor. He ate straight from the pick'n'mix display and now you must pay for sweets you didn't even let him have. Oh, great, now he's full of sugar, too.

That little sod has, say, two siblings, and they're starting to pick up on his behavior. Oh no, you say to yourself, one of them is bad enough. Sometimes, though you'll deny this to everyone, you question why you had him in the first place. You'll be damned if his siblings become little sods, too. So, what do you do? You punish the lot of them, right? That makes sense—by punishing the innocent children, you ensure that they will become the enforcers of your rules. Little Sod's reign of terror is over if he ever wants his siblings to talk to him again.

Kate Taylor, a very lovely thirty-something-year-old, had one of those little sods. His name was Bobby, and I hated his eight-year-old guts. He was one of those kids that just had to be heard … all … the … time. They could hear him on earth, and we could hear him in the damn, blasted heavens, too. His shrill little voice was always demanding something, and normally Kate caved immediately. That would cease the torrent of verbal stabbings to our eardrums, if only for a while.

Well, one day, Kate decided that enough was enough. She wasn't going to feel guilty about being a single parent with a single income anymore. Bobby needed discipline. And that's how it all started. He made a request—nay, a demand—and she refused him. This was the starting point for what's known on Earth as 'S' Day. Planet dwellers think the 'S' stands for 'soup', but we think it stands for 'sod'.

On that fateful day, I was lying in a cloud with my hands clasped over my ears, wondering why God had created Bobby Taylor in the first place. Not that I'm one to question the Lord, but I think if He were being honest, He'd admit that Bobby Taylor was a mistake.

You see, kids have a system; when they want something, they ask a parent. When that parent refuses, they go to the other parent, then their most gullible grandparent. If neither the second parent nor the grandparent options are available, they turn to Santa. *But what if it's not Christmas*, I hear you ask? Well, in that case, they start praying. And why wouldn't they? They're taught that God hears all their prayers, that He loves all his children and that He performs miracles.

When Kate refused Bobby's request for chicken soup (out of principle—it wasn't even lunch time), he bypassed all other routes and went straight for the big guy. He started praying. Relentlessly.

God was having a bad day at the office; it was a classic case of too many prayers and not enough time; there was a war that was … well, mid-war; some terrible virus was making the rounds; the Big Brother final was coming up and that's always a busy one.

So, you can imagine how annoying Bobby's steady stream of requests was. They were coming in fast and loud, interrupting other prayers, putting God off His train of thought, and generally causing a nuisance.

God tried to mute him, but it was no good; Bobby was determined to be heard. He was a loud kid in general, but when he wanted something, man, he could be persistent. We could all hear him way up in the clouds:

*Dear God, I really love chicken soup, please send me a lifetime's supply.*

*Dear God, I'm hungry for chicken soup.*

*God, why aren't you answering me?*

*G, where's my soup at?*

*Oh Goooodddddd, I know you can heeeeeear meeeeee.*

And then the kicker: *Dear God, if you loved me, you'd send me the soup I asked for.*

I took one look at God's face and knew that the planet was doomed. Ten plagues aside, God can normally control his temper, but man, that little sod. You wouldn't believe how often He hears "If you love me, then you'll…". It drives him absolutely bonkers.

"That little sod." God said, massaging his temples. "If he wants chicken soup, I'll give him chicken soup!"

And so, it rained.

At first, Bobby was excited when he felt the warm splash from above on his skin. He got more excited still when he licked it off his arm and declared that it was raining his favorite canned food. But then it poured, and it poured just on Bobby. Gallons of the stuff.

The kid tried to run, but you try running across chicken soup-covered ground. It got really slippery really fast, and the next thing he knew, Bobby was arse over tit in a considerably sized puddle of creamy goodness. Then came the lumps of chicken the size of which you've never seen. All right, they weren't lumps. They were whole chickens. Frozen ones.

You can imagine what frozen chickens falling from the sky can do to a skull. Especially when, technically speaking, they're not falling but rather being thrown like javelins from the arm of the Almighty.

That was the end of Bobby Taylor. It would have been the end of the whole episode if Kate Taylor had just kept her trap shut. God had had his fun, he'd vented some frustration, and he'd rid the world of the biggest little sod there was.

I'm sure you can sympathize with the Holy One when I tell you that Kate Taylor kicked off. I know what you're thinking: most parents would, right? She made this big fuss in front of the spectators who'd witnessed the chicken-skull fiasco. She claimed that Bobby was taken before his time, that God was an unfair so-and-so, and that she was turning her back on Him forever. I suppose any parent would, but the thing was, when God oh-so-literally answered Bobby's prayer, he was answering Kate's too.

The whole time we could hear Bobby rambling about his soup, we could all hear a very faint but persistently pleading cry for help from Kate. I'm sure, looking back on it now, that she used the phrase "just kill the little fu—", well, you can fill in the rest. As soon as she saw those chickens come down, she smiled. We all saw it.

She was happy about it. And then she had the gall to stand there wailing that it was a tragedy. Well, that really tied God in a knot. So, He kept raining soup and He kept throwing chickens.

Remember that parent I mentioned earlier, the one who punishes all their children for the crimes of one? Yeah, so that's what happened. Bobby started the fire, Kate wafted the flames, and God put it out. For forty days and nights, the people of Earth endured warm soup splashes and frozen chicken-related deaths.

When the puddles started to coalesce into lakes, we tried to stop Him, but He was in no mood to be told what to do. He had had it with the trivial prayers, expectations, and complaints from His children. I tried to tell Him that they had learned their lesson, and that perhaps flooding the world with soup was a little overboard (da da dum). His reply was that to prove that He loves his children equally, He has to treat them all the same. If one needs a good smiting, then they all do.

The results of the flood were bad for the majority. As you can imagine, due to the lack of warning, there was no time to build an ark. There wasn't even enough time to assemble a raft, though a few did manage to assemble some inflatables.

That's not to say that there weren't any survivors, though humanity has taken a somewhat bizarre turn. In a thousand years or so, I can't wait to see what future humans will make of the cave drawings of those falling chickens.

Bobby, the absolute sod, has gone down in history as a martyr. Yeah, we couldn't believe it either.

With each of God's lessons, humanity takes something valuable away to progress with, but in this case, they were left a little perplexed. Scholars continue to try to make sense of 'S' Day, but the only conclusion drawn so far is that chicken soup is now banned. I'm hoping that the next little sod prays for carrots; I can't stand carrots.

# IOTA

# 10 AQUALUNG

## Anne Carly Abad

There, a planet gated away
under a lattice of roots and branches
from an Elder Tree—so old it's turned to stone—
the Lord of Earth must be warning us: stay back.
But our wings are weary, fleeing from
the fiery expansion, nowhere to perch
among the molten rocks of space
and the temperamental stars.

I shatter the Elder's limbs
and we mount the soil below
only to have the land curse us,
cause our pinions to fall,
fall like the rain that has begun to surge
from unseen clouds and banks above.
Taking our flight is not enough.
The earth requires flesh.

But then I find that water is kind
to those who drown,
cradling the damned in softness,
quieting the will to strive.

I float in the crystalline blue,
and count my siblings
asleep and bloated, becoming faceless...
my fingers are not enough.
The deluge becomes our bed
and the weight of water
our blanket. I hold on to
the boulder hands of a Nephilim
before peace washes over me
and I inhale cleansing liquid.

It fills my chest with slumber.
In my dream, the water lurches,
bending the membranes of my lungs.
It pulls at my skin, creating a flap.
It pushes back muscles until they split
and I awake, beating filaments and lamellae.

I am an angel of the sea.
The lord above banishes us to the depths,
but we have never perished.

SHORT STORIES

# 11 FIELDS OF THE NEPHILIM

## Alex S. Johnson

When the Nephilim fell from heaven, they burned the skies, their dark wings spreading across the miles, their feet driving the bones of the previous angels further into the soil.

In those days, there was much bewilderment and wonder among the people, for creatures of pure metaphysics had been raining for decades and they were sore afraid of being sore afraid and sick unto death of being sick unto death. The bones of the angels moldered in the earth and spread contagion laterally and strange plants vertically, which shot up in the form of sharp-edged musical instruments that the people did play upon. In those days, also, many gods battled for the single position available, and the people lacked such knowledge and discernment that would enable them to pick one heavenly leader among the contenders. As they awaited that day, they plucked lutes and harps and guitars and blew upon trumpets that evoked storms of blood and desolating tornadoes that churned the land.

The Nephilim were big-boned and frankly scary to the people of Earth, and when they demanded luscious maidens, the people of Earth had no recourse but to surrender their daughters, saying, please, whatever you do, don't get giants upon them, for those giants are creepy and malignant.

Hearing their cries but being not of Earth, the Nephilim said unto them, Ha, it will be our greatest pleasure to plow your daughters like unto the fields and produce all the giants we want. And what will thou doest with thy puny limbs and lutes and harps and guitars, form an army of little ones, the least of whom will not stand up to the feet of a giant and the greatest of whom will at most reach half of half a knee's height? For the Nephilim were cocksure and desperately horny for the daughters of Earth and intent upon creating giants, which was their pastime in those days.

And the people of Earth said to Moses, Dude, what in the fuck have we done to incur the wrath of the gods, such that they continue to plague us with storms and tornadoes and fallen angels and more fallen angels and now these huge-winged psychopaths who crave our daughters for the purpose of making giants upon them?

And some in their desperation formed cults, either to placate the many gods or to placate those leaders who had grown among them with mighty claims to power. And these cults did proliferate until all the people of Earth either belonged to them or were excluded; but as the people of Earth were fewer then than they are now, most were able to join at least one cult. And these cults did excommunicate, condemn, and ostracize all other cults, and there was much fighting among the people and infighting among members of the cults.

Meanwhile, the fall of the Nephilim continued. Among the daughters of the people of Earth were the first Hos, called the Hohim, who craved the colossal tools of the Nephilim and did suck upon them until the skies were full unto whiteness with the sperm that did spurt. The Nephilim plowed and plundered and ravished these daughters and made baby giants that did howl and scream and curse and throw their scat like unto a great shitstorm. And the heavens were smeared with excrement and spunk and blood and other bodily products and darkened the skies. The cults then took of the sperm and shit and blood and made monstrous protectors from them that were called Golem. And while there were some who looked upon the psychotic confusion that reigned upon Earth and said whoa, the gods will be displeased with this situation and curse us and despise us and sow dissension among us and make of us little butt-slaves, the leaders of the cults cried Ha, for they were drunk with power and had also imbibed of the Kool-Aid that did shower from the cocks of Golem.

And this Kool-Aid was of such potency and hallucinogenic effect that it shattered what little rationality did prevail among the peoples of Earth, and the first age of Full-Bore Batshit Crazy began.

The Nephilim became bored with the demands and pleas and shrieks and cries and heinous fuckery of the daughters and they sought other delights such as were provided by the Kool-Aid. And they too drank of that evil drink, as did the Golem, who then formed a collective. And this collective sought to exterminate, drive out and repulse all those who had not drunk thereof and become flushed with strange thoughts that led them to ritual practices that were an abomination to at least seven generations (for the accounting in those days was not rigorous and seven generations could be translated into four, or five, or twenty-two of ours today).

By the end of the first age of Full-Bore Batshit Crazy, all the people of Earth and their daughters and sons and nephews and cousins were sick again of being sick and tired of the constant wars that raged unabated until five only were left of the people of Earth and the Nephilim were in rout and the daughters were simply hot messes and no longer even cute in a beer goggles way. The bodily wastes that filled the sky had blocked the sun and now the Earth began to freeze, and the peoples of Earth sought caves.

In these caves they drew—rough sketches at first, then more detailed artwork, and finally, glorious masterpieces that would be an example unto many more generations if the Earth did not then vomit forth creatures that were slimy confabulations of all the angels, demons, whores, magical trumpets and lutes and drums and very slutty whores that were called the New Hohim, and the art became labored and crude again and finally like unto clods of crap. And because they were hungry and thirsty the people ventured forth into the freezing air and made weapons with which to slay these creatures and make of them nourishment and sustenance. But the creatures were so foul and awful that even when they had been cooked into charcoal blocks, they were still inedible, and the last peoples of Earth turned on one another, regardless of cult affiliation, and cannibalism reigned.

And the God who was the true God and not a half-assed pretender such as were the many, many false gods who had planted their flags in the Earth, the God whose patience was great and whose mercy for his creation was overwhelming, finally had had enough. And he summoned the angels that were not fakes or frauds or phonies and He said unto them, the shit, it hath finally gotten real. And they bowed and gesticulated and humbled themselves before the one God (accept no substitutes) and said unto Him that was on high, how can we rectify the great confusion and outright weirdness that now baffles even the greatest minds of Earth and Heaven and outlying regions?

And the one God who wasn't that other guy or him either or that fat little man who wears of the mask and dispenses the Kool-Aid from his throne of shit said, well, I dunno. I thought I might send plagues and boils and hateful critters and wrath and other forms of heinous fuckery to they that are of Earth, but even if I do so, they have very little self-respect or hope left and would probably sit upon the ground and take of it like unto a little bitch that is a ho. And He thought some more and finally he said, take of the shit and sperm and blood and form stars and planets and, dammit, a real cosmos that is far greater than anything these miserable humans have seen, and fling the Nephilim to the farthest spheres, and show the people of Earth light and reason. And the angels heard these words which could not be heard by human ears without great implosion, and they came upon the Earth to check out the situation thereof.

And they saw the peoples of Earth were huddled in their caves, quaking and shaking and imprecating and still worshipping numerous abominations and demons and they saw also that these people were scared out of their ever-loving minds, and they knew not what to do. And the angels took pity on them and drew them out of their caves and showed them the many things they could do with their hands and feet and minds and hearts and other organs and attributes belonging to them. And while the vast majority maintained the bitterness that had grown like a disease contaminating every cell, a few listened to the gentle advice of the angels and started to plant seeds that grew into a mighty rain forest. And rain dropped upon the Earth and the skies began to clear of the stink that stanketh and even a few of the Hohim repented and the men of Earth were exceeding glad because they had grown ill of the sexually-transmitted diseases that made of their members to rot and fall off.

And for a very brief period there was peace on Earth. A very, very brief period, but a period, nonetheless.

# 12 DREAMERS OF THE DELUGE

## Allen Ashley

Uncle Saul could hear well enough for himself but nevertheless told David, "Have a look outside the door, kid, see if it's still raining."

David briefly poked his head through the gap and came back inside with drops of water falling off his hair and nose.

"I'll take that as a yes," Saul stated. "Reckon the valley must be flooded by now."

"I'd say fifty cubits high and rising. It'll soon flood us out, Uncle Saul. I hope Rebekah's safe. And her family."

"Still pining after that shy one, eh? She's a bit young for you, ain't she?"

"Just by a year. She's on the cusp of womanhood."

"The what? Where'd you learn to talk like that? You been hanging out with that crazy rabbi, Shimon?"

They fell silent for a while. The rain now pounded against the wooden planks atop their shelter. From the attached lean-to, their animals moaned softly against the divine punishment. David had started to lose track of time. He was not sure whether it was afternoon or evening. The dark sky and the dim fog inside the building gave no real clues either way. He took a few more bites from their small store of unleavened bread even though he wasn't particularly hungry. Then he needed to take a few sips of water from their shared stone bowl. It seemed a little absurd—if he was really thirsty, he could just stick his head through the doorway and open his mouth to the liquid descending sky.

Saul's eyes shone in the shadows. His teeth, too, despite a predilection for the fruit of the vine. "Reckon we missed a trick with that carpenter guy, Noah," he said.

"Neighbor of your lovely betrothed, Rebekah," he added.

"She's not my betrothed, Uncle. Maybe one day. But what do you mean, 'missed a trick?'"

"We should be on his boat, David, ready to ride out the waves of outrageous fortune."

"He wasn't taking passengers, Uncle. Only his family and two each of every kind of animal."

"Exactly. Two of each. There ain't just one kind of human, you know, just like there ain't just one kind of fish. With your dark hair and my weather-worn face, we could have said we were Levites. Or from Samaria. Egypt, at a push. I've been there, I speak some of the language. Lovely lingo, especially from the mouths of some of the harlots I met 'round the back of Alfalfa Market."

"Uncle! You shouldn't!"

"Because you never have? I bet you've thought about it, though, and I bet you're intending to if we make it out of this downpour in one piece."

"Uncle, it's sin that God is punishing. You know that. Mr. Noah told us so."

Maybe he was still too young to really know what he was talking about. His body had started to change over the past year, sprouting hairs in private and not-so-private places. He would wake with his bedcover wet from his less-than-holy dreams. He was sure that Rebekah must be undergoing some similar sort of transformation beneath the thick covering of clothing that her parents made her habitually wear even in the hot Galilean summer. God was punishing the earth for its sinfulness and—blasphemous thought—perhaps his brutal hand was being too all-inclusive in washing away all transgressors. *I don't deserve to die,* David thought. *I've never done no fornicating. Maybe I've thought of it, but men should be judged on their actions. That's what's fair. If the Lord can get inside your head like the holy men claimed, maybe he should spend some time fixing our thinking. Next, he'll be punishing me for my dreams.*

He'd had a dream last week that he and Rebekah ran away to Egypt to grow crops by the fertile Nile. He'd told Uncle Saul, who'd commented, "If that deluge arrives, the whole world's gonna become the Nile, boy."

His thoughts were interrupted by a slight lessening of the percussive precipitation above which he could hear the tethered animals braying.

"Why don't we bring the beasts inside?" Saul said. "May come in useful."

They had tethered the goat and the donkey very loosely with just a rope thrown over a stick so that if the creatures had any wherewithal, they could make their own escape through the omnipresent downpour. David was a little surprised that neither had done so. They had some sort of lingering loyalty to their human masters.

Soaked to the skin, he led the smaller creature into the shelter. It gave off a fecund, wet smell. Was it his uncle's intention to use these as a final food source?

"Reckon it's up to sixty cubits now," Saul stated. "Almost lapping at the entrance. You ready to swim for it?"

"Of course. I've swum all my life. Caught fish that way. No need of a net."

"Good lad. This rain is going to bring the fish right into our laps, of course. Or take us into their realm. Whichever way you want to look at it."

David remembered his father lowering him into the clear water when he was a mere toddler, encouraging him to be at ease in this element. His late father had been a fisherman, and his father before him. As he struggled to cope with the taboo-testing exposures of puberty, David had often doused himself in the cooling waters. Last week he thought he had espied someone else at the far shore, but the hot sun confused his eyes, and he couldn't be certain. Now it was a requirement that they all be swimmers.

The cramped space was suddenly lit from without by a brilliant flash of lightning and, ten seconds afterwards, a body shuddering clap of thunder. Noah's scientific descendants would have used this information to calculate that the angry center of Heaven was two miles distant. For now.

"Ah, that's what's been missing all along," Saul said, "our creator's roar. Time to make a move, I believe."

"We're not going out into that, are we?"

"Suit yourself, sunshine. I'm not remaining here to watch the last few fingers of air disappear as the flood reaches the roof. Come on, choose your mount. No, on second thoughts, you're much lighter than me. You take the goat, I'll get on the donkey."

David knew that Uncle Saul would have preferred an Arabian horse. Two years back, he had returned from his travels with one in tow, and for a while the beast had proven to be a boon to his family's farm laboring. But a loose stone had led to an infected foot, and they had reluctantly stabbed it out of its misery. Unsure of the dietary teachings of the Torah, they had secretly cooked its flesh and feasted upon its goodness for a week. That was back when the weather was dry and predictable, and life went on much as it had done for generations…

"Stop dawdling, David."

"I don't think the goat's strong enough."

"Nonsense. You're still a mere slip of a thing. Get on, the water's up to our knees already."

All around, all ahead of and behind them now was water. Their shepherd shelter survived maybe a minute longer before being submerged. It was as if they were out on the wild sea with no land in sight. Already, it was hard to remember that this had once been farms, plantations, fishing lakes, homes, and habitations. The irate sky fell upon them. The goat struggled to keep itself afloat as well as free itself of its human burden. To David's right, his uncle atop the donkey fared slightly better, riding one-handed as if born to the semi-aquatic life.

"Let's keep going until we fall off the end of the world," Saul called.

Lust, envy, greed, and gluttony—Saul had indulged in many a sin during his happier days, but the greatest of his crimes was surely pride. The cloud-enclosed sky darkened momentarily above their sodden figures, then a sudden shaft of light like an inspiration pierced the gloom. But no, it was forked. David felt it as a tingle through his whole body, losing consciousness momentarily before recovering to feel somehow changed, his muscles aching more than he could have conceived. Of his companion and the two animals, there was no sign. He had no time to dwell upon their saturated fate as the waves swelled, and he set about swimming as he had been taught, as he had always done, and as he must do until exhaustion claimed his soul. All his years of practice in the lake at Galilee had prepared him for this moment, but he knew that he didn't have the strength to keep going for hours, for days, for who knew how long? Only God knew, and he was the source of this deluge.

He kicked through the water. He strove to stay afloat. He placed one arm forward, then the other in a beautiful symmetry that might, under other circumstances, have gained him some admiring and shy glances. Though the rain smeared his vision and dripped down hair, cheeks, eyes and nose, David regulated his breathing as much as he could. His gaze scanned the horizon for any outcrop of rock, building, or tall tree that might still hold its head above the surface and provide a brief respite. There was nowhere towards the direction of sunrise. Letting his body be turned by the swirl, he set out for the direction he knew as sunset, reflecting bitterly that he and the rest of humankind had doubtless had their last ever sighting of the celestial orb. He kept going. The survival instinct stayed strong. He kicked with both legs together, and his arms ploughed through the unquiet water. After a while, he was barely able to feel the pain of effort. He would hold onto this precious life for as long as he could even without hope or any sign of salvation.

Finally, there was a suggestion of a break in the surface some hundred cubits ahead. Did his eyes deceive him? No, it looked like land. Keep swimming; don't give up now.

Yes, miraculously, there were rocks here above the water. Oh, to rest, if only for a heartbeat or three.

And there, like a vision, was Rebekah, sitting atop the outcrop, brushing her dark hair loose with a comb of bone and with her breasts bare. So brazen. What had made her act like this? But these were changed times. Clothes would slow her down and drag her under the roiling water. God, she was beautiful! All his youthful dreams personified.

As his tired strokes degenerated somewhat, he struggled to keep focused on staying afloat but was drawn inexorably towards this vision in front of him. The rainwater rolled down her smooth torso, making her appear like a figure created by pigments, not quite in focus, ready to be washed away at any moment. Wait for me, my betrothed.

She suddenly became aware of David's plight and threw down her comb so that she could help drag him up to this temporary refuge. As he struggled to control his labored breathing, he saw that Rebekah no longer had legs. His addled brain wondered, had she ever? He was sure she had, as a little girl. Although of late, he'd never seen her without heavy garments. Instead, she now possessed a tail. She smiled. As he tried to rise, he realized that he could no longer stand in the old way because his legs, too, had fused into a tail. The wrathful lightning had left its mark.

"Come, David," she said, "the prophet Noah has said that two of each shall survive this flood. Look at me and gaze upon yourself. This is the divine miracle all those not on the Ark have craved. I believe the Lord has given us a new purpose. A change and a chance."

His uncle's words echoed through his head about there being more than one type of human. But this was surely stretching the definitions way past breaking point.

Rebekah—grown, confident, womanly—paid no heed to his indecision and conjecture. Half-human, half-fish, she dived headlong into the water. He watched the ripples for a moment then followed her.

# 13 THE IMMERSION OF THE INCORPOREUM

## AmyBeth Inverness

Moesha loved the rain. Her uncle wouldn't make her work in the field during a storm, and her Aunt said she only got in the way inside. The rain was Moesha's escape. She'd run through the drops, not caring that she was soaked to the skin. That summer she'd bled for the first time, and her uncle had found a man eager for another young bride. Never mind that the first three had died … Moesha's uncle was just glad to be rid of her.

The rain didn't last long. She looked at her feet, the same color as the mud that coated them. A tiny cascade ran over the rocks and into the puddle. The Cascade spoke to her. "Stay … just a little while longer. A few more minutes won't hurt."

So, Moesha stayed. The rain began again, harder this time. Moesha watched the water, heedless that she was soaked to the skin. The water caressed her. No human ever had or ever would. She held no fantasies about the man who would be her husband. She would die, either at his hand or bearing his child.

The Cascade caressed her. When she did finally return home, she slipped in without waking the others and fell asleep listening to the comforting sound of the rain.

#

"The water is so quiet," Visola said. She wasn't used to water being quiet. Water was noisy and raucous. She was surrounded by an ocean of it, yet the only sounds were from the other passengers and crew.

"It's peaceful," Maggie said. "Water and I have always been friends. Did I tell you they pulled me and my cradle out of a flood when I was a baby?"

Visola snorted. Everyone knew the story of the unsinkable Maggie Brown. She was one of the lucky few who got to hear it from the woman herself. "Yes. And the story gets more and more fantastic each time you tell it."

Maggie laughed. "Well, then, your turn to tell me a wild story. One of your past lives …"

"Moesha? The girl who watched Noah build the ark?"

"That one doesn't have a happy ending. Neither does that one who was drowned as a witch—"

"Ondine?"

"Ondine. Pretty name. Sad story." Maggie accepted a glass of fruit punch from a passing waiter. "How about the one in the hurricane?"

Visola nodded, accepting a glass of punch for herself. For a moment she thought the waiter was ignoring her, most likely due to the color of her skin, but then he smiled and offered her a drink. "Nixie. Nixie the nitwit."

Maggie laughed. "Now, now, one mustn't speak ill of the dead."

"I apologize. But she would have lived a lot longer if she hadn't been such a nitwit …"

#

Nixie watched the weather channel with interest. The storm was building strength, and it would hit soon. She probably had a day at most to pack and get out of town. Her sister was already hosting several family members who had decided to evacuate early.

Nixie had no intention of evacuating. The Lord had given her a beautiful home, and she knew He would not take it away. It was her reward for working all those hours at the food pantry.

A frantic barking called her to the back door. She opened it and two dachshunds scampered in. It was starting to rain. "Oh, this is just a warm-up," Nixie said. "The big storm will be here tomorrow."

The dogs wagged their tails and looked up at her in adoration. Nixie checked her supply of puppy treats. She was prepared for the long haul. Food, bottled water, an emergency radio.

She'd get through the storm just fine.

#

Nixie is a terrible listener. I've tried poking at her loneliness and making her want to see her sister and family, but that only makes her more stubborn. I've warned her that this hurricane will flood her neighborhood and the entire parish. So, what does she do? She buys candles. Not just utility ones either. She buys jars that are scented with the smells of the beach.

In a few days, this whole place will smell like the beach. And not in a good way.

I stretch out from Nixie and can't decide which way to go—forwards or backwards? I wish I could flip a coin. No opposable thumbs, no fingers, no body. Anyway …

Back … back this time. Through Visola, who is asleep, listening to the sound of the gentle waves as the ocean liner cruises through the frigid water. Past Ondine, who was drowned in the witch trials. Back further …

Moesha is a good listener. She converses with me. She calls me Cascade because she hears my voice in the water. Who am I to argue with that name? I think it's pretty.

My Beloved is scared, but she does not tremble. She knows her life will be short, though she thinks it will be at the hands of the man she is contracted to marry.

I could help Nixie, but she won't listen. Visola is strong, though that might be her doom. I couldn't save Ondine. I was the reason they thought she was a witch. I can't help Moesha, even though she hears me clearly. But I can comfort her.

"It will rain soon," I say. Moesha is nursing her blistered fingers. Her Aunt was not happy with the last bushel Moesha brought in, but she no longer beats her. I think she wants to make sure Moesha isn't black and blue when she is married. I guess blistered fingers aren't a problem.

"Would you like me to fetch water?" Moesha asks.

Her Aunt looks annoyed, but she says yes and shoos us away. By the time we reach the well, a gentle rain is falling. Moesha fills the bucket and returns it to the tent. Then we slip away to where no one will bother us.

"Why is he building such a large … thing?" Moesha asks me.

"Noah? He is Beloved of The Word. He is doing what God wants him to do."

"Beloved? Like me? Does he have a friend inside him?"

I look towards the yard where Noah and his sons are hard at work. "I don't think so," I answer. I've never been close enough to see if others of my kind are there.

"What about the others?" Moesha asks.

"I don't know," I answer honestly. "Possibly."

Moesha watches them with keen interest. "Do you think they are almost finished?"

I squeeze Moesha's soul gently, then dart out and back again. I do not like to be away from her, even for a moment, but I am curious, as well. "They hurry because they know the rain will come soon," I tell Moesha.

My Beloved looks up at the clouds, drops bouncing off her cheeks. "It is raining now!"

I hold My Beloved and comfort her. I want to take the peace and contentment she feels now and give it back to her when it is time. "Yes, this little sprinkle, it is raining now. But soon …"

#

"How did Nixie know when the storm was going to hit?" Maggie asked.

Visola concentrated, trying to remember. That was the strangest part about her past life, the box with the screen. Moving pictures and sound. It was called a 'television.' It was only one of many things about Nixie's life Visola didn't understand.

"She heard a news report," Visola said. It was the best explanation she had. Saying that the weatherman had a magic screen that showed pictures of the storm from high in the sky above the clouds made it sound like some fantasy from Jules Verne.

The television was not the strangest memory she had of her past lives. She never told Maggie about Niloufer, who lived in a cave. She never told anyone. Niloufer *was* someone out of a Jules Verne fantasy, and Visola had no explanation for the memories she had.

When Niloufer came out of her cave and looked to the horizon, she saw a bleak landscape, not a single tree or bush anywhere in sight. And in the sky, hovering on the horizon, was not the moon …

It was Earth.

#

"Niloufer, have you checked the levels in catch-basin four?" Jo called from somewhere above.

Niloufer looked out over the surface of the water. So much in one place, enough to immerse herself. Enough to immerse fifty people. "Three centimeters higher than yesterday," she shouted. "It's working!"

Thirty years they'd been mining the polar ice. Thirty years, and they'd barely provided enough to keep up with the growing demand as more and more colonists arrived to find their fortune on the moon.

"Over there!" Cascade whispered to her.

Niloufer moved around the narrow ledge. It was a natural basin, and footholds were an afterthought. She could hear it, but she couldn't see it yet. An actual drip. Multiple drips! Running water, coming from the rock above, filling the catch-basin with life-giving water.

She shone her light on the rocks where the sound was coming from. Sure enough, a drizzle of water was coming from a small fissure in the wall. She reached out to touch it, but the ledge was too narrow. She couldn't risk falling in. For a child born on the moon, there were no swimming lessons, no summers at the lake. Those were stories her parents told from their youths on Earth. Niloufer had never seen their home planet other than when she took an excursion to the surface. From their vantage point at the moon's southern pole, Earth was perpetually on the horizon, playing peek-a-boo with her since she was a baby.

"Niloufer?" Jo called again. "Are you coming up any time soon?"

"Soon!" Niloufer said, giving up trying to reach the drizzle. "Very soon."

#

"Soon?" Moesha asked, splaying her fingers, palms upwards, watching the raindrops dance on her hands.

"Soon the rains will come heavier and heavier," Cascade explained gently. "Soon, soon the waters will cover the land."

Moesha laughed. "Water covering the land? Uncle won't like that. He won't like that at all."

Cascade embraced her Beloved. She wanted to explain. She wanted to make Moesha understand, but it wouldn't make any difference.

Soon.

#

"What on God's green earth was that?" Maggie asked. It was shortly before midnight and the crowd was raucous.

"What was what?" Visola asked. She could hardly hear anything over the singing and shouting.

"I'll go find out," said one of the younger gentlemen.

Visola had almost forgotten about him when he returned a half hour later. "I don't mean to alarm you ladies, but the ship has hit an iceberg! The captain has ordered the lifeboats deployed. I'll see you safely there."

The change in the crowd was surreal. Some, in the heart of the crush, still had no idea what was going on, while others were hastily gathering their things and heading out to the deck. Maggie was at the door, people pushing past her. "Visola? We need to go."

Visola looked around her. The crowd was quickly figuring out that *something* was wrong, even if they had no idea what. Visola hurried to Maggie's side. "Should we get our things?" she asked, watching a man dragging a very large trunk towards the edge of the deck.

Maggie shook her head. "There's nothing in my cabin I can't replace. A fortune in fabrics, perhaps, but I needed to buy a new wardrobe anyway."

Visola tried to keep up, but the crush of the crowd separated her from

Maggie. The last she saw was the plume of Maggie's feathered hat reach a lifeboat, and Visola gave up trying to stay close to her friend.

"No! Don't leave me! You can't!" a young woman clutching an infant was screaming at a man. A toddler was clinging to her skirts.

"You must take the children and go to a lifeboat. Now!" the man said. He gave her a swift kiss on the cheek and ran off.

"No!" the woman screeched and ran after him. The toddler fell, crying even harder. Visola scooped him up and caught up to the wailing woman, grabbing her by the skirt.

"Madam, please—" Visola started to say, but the woman collapsed in her arms. Visola held her awkwardly, trying to make sure neither the toddler nor the baby was crushed in the embrace. "Madam, we need to get to a lifeboat."

It took an eternity to get the woman to calm down enough to move. When they finally reached a lifeboat, the sailor in charge looked at them. "We can only take one more." he said.

"Take her. And the babes. She's a tiny slip of a thing, and the children weigh nothing."

The sailor tried to say something, but Visola was already handing the woman and her children into the lifeboat. With a splash, it was out of her reach. The woman looked up, clutching her babies to her. Visola hoped the woman would continue to hold them tight.

#

Nixie huddled on the couch with the dogs. There was a thin sheet of water covering the yard, and it was still raining heavily.

Someone pounded on the door. "Anyone in there? We need to evacuate immediately."

The dogs gave her away, howling and scampering off to bark through the picture window while standing on the back of the couch. Nixie opened the door before the men decided to break it down. "Thank you for your concern, but we're just fine where we are. It's safer inside. You two just move on and find someone who needs your help. The Good Lord is watching over me."

She closed the door, but the man just banged again, even louder. "Ma'am, you can't stay here. It's not safe."

Nixie missed the rest of what he was saying. She scooped up the dogs and turned off the television, then headed upstairs. Maybe this storm was going to be worse than she thought, but that didn't change anything. The Lord had blessed her with a beautiful home, and she was going to stay.

#

Moesha runs through the rain. "Is this it?" she asks. "Is this the rain that will cover the world?"

"Yes," I tell her. I am sad, but Moesha is not. This is her wedding day, but there will be no wedding. The rain is coming down so hard that even the livestock has been brought inside. Moesha is the only living being in sight.

"Do you think they'll fight? All those animals?" she asks me. I know she is talking about the ark. We watched all the animals climb on board, seemingly more than such a vessel could possibly hold, but that is the way of The Word.

"No. They do not fight," I say. Moesha's feet are covered now. She splashes as if it was a puddle, but the water covers the ground.

I wonder if we should go higher, perhaps find some rock to cling to. But it will not make a difference. It is more important that Moesha remain at peace.

#

"Calm down, babies, calm down. Everything will be all right." Nixie looked at the water, halfway up the stairs. "Here, have another treat."

The dogs refused to eat. They huddled on the bed, shivering with cold, barking whenever there was a strange noise.

*Open the window*, said that strange voice in her head. Sometimes the voice was helpful. Other times, like the present, it was not.

The dogs ran to the window and barked excitedly. It was a French window that opened onto a tiny porch, one of her favorite features about the house. A light was shining up.

Nixie peered through the glass, but she couldn't see anything. It was dark, and the rain was still coming down heavily. She hadn't had electricity for hours, though she had every flashlight and lantern she owned turned on in the bedroom.

*Open the window!* said the voice more insistently.

"Fine," Nixie grumbled, opening the latch and bracing herself as the wind blew both sides wide open. A light shone directly in her eyes.

"Ma'am! Are you all right? Is anyone else there with you?" said a voice from below.

*JUMP!* said the voice inside her.

Both dogs jumped. "Baby! Princess! No!" Nixie wailed, hearing splashes from below.

The light left her eyes and shone on the water. Her babies were paddling frantically. "Don't worry, we've got them," said the man in the boat.

"Are they all right?" Nixie shouted.

"They're both scared stiff, but they're fine. Can you climb down? Is there another window closer to the water where you can climb out?"

Nixie looked down at her nightgown. She certainly wasn't dressed to go anywhere. "Just a minute," she said. She found the box of doggie treats, then saw the birthday card her sister had sent her. The envelope had her sister's address. She put the envelope in the box and hurried back to the window. "Here, they'll need these," Nixie said, tossing the box down to the boat. "My sister's address is inside. Just send the puppies there. I'll go pick them up when this is all over."

"Ma'am! You need to evacuate …"

Nixie couldn't hear any more. She closed the window and climbed back into bed. It was lonely without the dogs, but they would be better off waiting out the storm at her sister's house up north.

#

Visola jumped into the water. She had checked both sides of the ship twice. There were no more lifeboats. She had stopped to help a young boy who was separated from his parents, finally loading him into a lifeboat and promising she would go find them. After a half hour, she decided it was a promise she could not keep. There was too much chaos.

She could see lifeboats with dim lights not far from the ship. Most of them were inexplicably half empty. The water was calm, and she was a strong swimmer. Growing up in Port-au-Prince, she practically lived in the water.

The waters of Port-au-Prince were warm and inviting. The icy ocean hit her like a sledgehammer, and Visola gasped as she reached the surface. Every nerve in her body cried out in pain, begging her to get out of the frigid water. She forced herself to move, but all she could manage was a weak doggie paddle. There were blurry lights ahead, and she tried to reach them.

A terrible noise rent the night and Visola turned to see the Titanic ship, one end raised far out of the water, the other immersed in the waves. Slowly, the uppermost section peeled away, the ship split in two, and the upper section fell with a crash into the water. Visola felt herself being sucked under, and she didn't have the strength to fight it.

She opened her eyes and saw Ondine before her, arms and legs bound. She closed her eyes, opened her mouth, and let out her last gasp of air.

#

Niloufer climbed down the ladder to the ledge again. This time, it was covered in water. "Jo!" she called up. "It's already over the ledge!"

She wondered if she should just turn around and go back up. She felt guilty for putting her feet in the water, but she did need to find out, well, she needed to see the drip for herself. She needed to know if it was more than a trickle. It sounded like more than a trickle.

Niloufer carefully waded along the ledge. She shone her light ahead. There it was! A tiny waterfall, perfect and beautiful, cascading over the rocks and into the catch-basin. She laughed. "It's filling, Jo! Steady and perfect. We did it!"

Niloufer's feet went out from under her. She dropped her light, and it sank beneath the surface, illuminating the already substantial depth. She sputtered and tried to tread water. She couldn't find the ledge. It was dark, and the only light was the glow from below. She tried to shout for help but only succeeded in getting a mouthful of water.

Panic set in. Then, a moment later, peace.

#

Moesha is asleep now. She found a thick mattress of woven reeds. It floats, even with her on it. But it is cold, and this is the kind of sleep from which she will never wake. She is with me now.

Ondine's limbs are bound. She does not thrash. She accepts her fate, opening her lungs to the water and giving her life to the lake. I hold her hand

and we walk towards the light together.

Visola joins us. Her body is in the darkness now. Moesha takes her by the hand, smiling at her.

Nixie thrashes. She is cold, even though she is in her warm bed. But her blankets no longer comfort her. They bind her.

Ondine takes Nixie by the hand. She stops thrashing at last. She is confused.

I feel the million Beloveds within me as I am within them. We are all swimming, we are all floating, we are all immersed in the waters of life. Some are being born. Some are being baptized. Others are at the end of their lives. They are about to go where I cannot.

I reach for Niloufer. She has no idea what to do. Never has she seen enough water to immerse her entire body. The thing that will give life to her community is the very thing that is killing her.

I touch Niloufer. I comfort her.

"NO!"

It is Visola. She has turned from the light, letting go of Moesha's hand. Moesha turns, as well, watching.

"No!" Visola says, calling to Niloufer. "You may not be able to swim, but you can float!"

Niloufer stares at Visola, not understanding.

"Like this!" Moesha says. She shows Niloufer her body, lungs full, arms spread wide, bobbing on the surface.

Niloufer looks up. The next time her face breaks the surface she gasps for air and struggles to take in as much breath as she can. She turns, chest up, arms wide, forcing her head to stay back even though instinct is telling her to curl into a ball.

"No!" Visola says again. "Stay flat. They will find you."

#

Niloufer stared at the vision, but as soon as she managed to break the surface again, she forced herself to turn onto her back, thinking of her chest as a balloon that would keep the rest of her body afloat.

"Niloufer! Where are you?" Jo called.

Niloufer coughed. Her body buckled, and she began to sink beneath the surface again. She forced herself to calm down, arching her back and floating like the girl had shown her.

A light shone in her eyes. "Oh my god, she fell in! Beck, get me a rope!"

"I can swim," came a masculine voice. Beck, she presumed. Low on the totem pole in the company, but fresh from college on Earth.

"Niloufer, listen to me carefully. If you panic and grab me, we may both go under. I'm going to come out to you and tow you back to the edge. You don't need to answer me. Just trust me."

*Pretend you're a boat!* Cascade told her. Niloufer felt Beck's arm around her neck, and she tentatively placed her hands on his hand.

"It's all right. I've got you. Almost there."

Once she was safely out of the catch-basin, all Niloufer could think of was what a waste it was that so much water was drenching her clothes. She felt so stupid. Beck and Jo took her straight to the medical ward, where the doctor proclaimed her hale and hearty but told her to go home and get some rest.

A week later, Niloufer climbed into the tiny boat with Beck, both wearing inflatable vests. The water level was down again, as it was now being piped up to be filtered and used by the colonists.

"Where is it?" Beck asked.

*Over there!*

"Over there," Niloufer pointed.

Beck guided the boat over to where she had seen the trickle before. It was now a steady stream. Beck used a probe to insert a light into the waterfall.

"Does it look like that on Earth?" Niloufer asked.

"Sort of," Beck answered. "On Earth, there would be lots of plants growing around the water."

*Now over there!*

"Let's check over there next," Niloufer said, pointing farther along the rock wall.

Sure enough, there was another tiny waterfall feeding into the catch-basin. Beck inserted another light, and they continued around, finding a dozen sources that were producing water.

*Now ... over there ... farther ... and up ...*

"Let's look over there," Niloufer said.

"There? Back in the corner? I don't hear any running water from that direction."

Niloufer didn't hear it either, but she trusted Cascade.

*Here!*

Niloufer shone her light on the rock. It was wet, seeping, but not running.

"Well, miracles do happen," Beck said.

Niloufer shone her light in the same place he was. "What?" she asked.

"Look closely."

Somewhere high above, a hatch opened and closed, briefly illuminating the rock face just above them. There, clinging to the rocks, was a tiny vine. It was no more than a thread, but it was definitely organic, and definitely growing.

*Life finds a way.*

"Life finds a way, " Niloufer said, staring at the little miracle.

Beck nodded. "Indeed, it does."

# 14 REMNANTS OF THE FLOOD

## Gustavo Bondoni

The villagers looked at each other and smiled. The presence of foreigners, especially English-speaking foreigners, seemed to increase their determination to show everyone that they found nothing remarkable about the shaking. Their village had been trembling since before they were born and was no worse for wear, after all. Their grandfather's grandmothers had lived there forever.

But Bridget's team exchanged nervous glances. The shaking floor could easily have been explained by relatively mild or somewhat distant seismic activity, but it had been going on for days, and not a single seismograph anywhere else registered the movement. No, there was some kind of local event, and she just hoped it wasn't some nearby volcano about to let off a poisonous cloud or something.

"Bloody annoying, isn't it?" Peters remarked. It was obvious to everyone at the table that, like the villagers, he was also putting on a show, attempting to keep his tough guy image alive within the group. But he was as much a scientist as the rest, and he knew that villages didn't just shake for no reason.

Bridget looked around the table at the three men with her. Peters, his salt-and-pepper hair not quite as long as his beard, was the eldest by quite a margin, while Greg and Johnnie both looked too young to be doctoral candidates. Greg, the team's computer expert, was an overweight, red-headed Californian whose skin was so white that any exposure to the sun would probably kill him. Johnnie, on the other hand, was the perfect contrast: a black man from Brighton who was probably the fittest person she'd seen in years. He was perfect for any kind of fieldwork, with a mind as sharp as his body. But they were both too young.

She smiled at herself. At thirty-five, she wasn't even that old. So, when had she become the old fossil? Peters, of course, was older than she was, but his actual age seemed to be a state secret. He looked more like a mercenary veteran of some African bush war than a marine biologist from Sussex, and his eyes supported the impression.

"I hate it," Bridget said. If the men were going to insist on being macho, she was damned if she would play along. "Who ever heard of a village that shakes all the time?"

Johnnie laughed. "Who knows? Maybe the shaking village will be the biggest discovery of the trip. Don't you think it's strange that no one has studied it yet?"

"Oh, they probably studied it and studied it, but you'd have to dig through all those boxes to learn what they found," Peters observed flatly.

The boxes. That had been the most shocking find so far. The smiling guide at the National Archaeological Museum had shown them the warehouse with pride. "We've managed to preserve all the old files from the communist era. We've got people trying to get them typed into word processors and get them onto a database." It had turned out that "people" meant the guide herself and that, at the current rate, the job would take several decades. The woman just smiled and explained that that was a temporary situation, and that new funding wouldn't take long to arrive.

"Huh. We're probably repeating research they've done already." Greg said.

"Not bloody likely. Even the Russians only learned about the Black Sea flood after the wall came down. The Bulgarians probably learned about it in '96, just like everyone else."

"I bet they were happy," Greg replied. "Learning about it from Americans, of all things."

"I know some people at Oxford who weren't happy about it, either," the older man replied.

"Well, at least they're helping us now," Bridget interjected. "So, stop complaining."

Peters grunted. He liked to complain. "So, what do we do under the new conditions?"

She wasn't sure whether he was referring to the fact that the village seemed to shake like a rattle every half hour or so or whether he was complaining about something else. She decided to worry about it later. "We dive tomorrow, right on schedule. With any luck, we can find some evidence before it all gets shaken to bits."

#

There's a reason Bulgaria was never considered a prime holiday location. The rocky beach was home to just a few desultory bathers, and it was a wonder they were there at all, considering the fact that they shared the black stones with a wealth of plastic soft drink bottles, and especially since the day had dawned windy and a bit chilly for early June.

Their shaking little fishing village was about twenty miles north of Varna, its position marked not by a name on a map but by a kilometer marker. Presumably, it had a name once, but forty years of communism had erased it, and no one in the twenty years since had bothered to remedy the oversight. Not exactly the way to get hordes of middle-class Germans to patronize the seashore.

That same lack of people was precisely what had attracted Bridget's team. The beach and gently sloping seafloor beside the vibrating town was the perfect spot to search for clues of an ancient catastrophe, and they'd already uncovered plenty of evidence to support their theory. In fact, that day's objective was to ascertain whether a formation they'd found the day before actually was what it looked like.

They'd dived ten minutes before, carefully descending to the fifteen-meter depth, their beams illuminating the sediment floating in the murky water. "Not exactly the Red Sea, is it?" Peters remarked.

"Shut up and concentrate. We have sixty minutes of safe immersion left; let's use it for something more useful than discussing diving preferences," Bridget replied. She was unhappy enough that they were diving in a threesome instead of in two pairs, but the money just hadn't been there, and they needed Greg and his laptop up above, making sense of the sonar data. At least they'd accepted her extremely conservative time estimate without argument, and they'd submitted to training with intercom-equipped full face mask units with more enthusiasm than she'd expected. They understood when she told them that the university just hated losing researchers.

As if on cue, an American twang filled her head. She had the volume on the receiver turned up, but she would have to live with it. "You're right above the formation."

They dropped on her signal, sinking further into the soup-like water, until their light illuminated the bottom. Two beams found nothing but silt and sludge, but a third landed on a smallish, jagged shape. "To the northeast, now," Greg's voice told them. "You've drifted a bit."

They followed, and soon arrived. A small, regular pile of stones stood in front of them, the kind you'd find between old fields in any agricultural area in Europe. In any other setting, any group of scientists who weren't dedicated to the study of lichen would have passed by without a second glance. But here—

Silence reigned. Even Peters, always ready with a snide comment or a rude word, simply stared at the stones. Johnnie swam up to the wall and placed a hand on the nearest edge, as if it were some kind of religious carving. "Do you realize what this means?" he whispered into his mike.

"Yeah," Peters replied, "It means we can add another mystery to our list. I can see the base of that wall, which means it's about four feet high. If it's really seven thousand years old, it should be completely buried in silt."

"What's going on down there?" Greg's voice came in from above. "What can you see?" They ignored him and thought about what Peters had said.

"Who cares?" Johnnie asked. "What difference does it make?"

"Well, I've got these perfectly good explosives."

A burst of bubbles floated up as Johnnie laughed at the joke, but Bridget wasn't inclined towards mirth. Peters would be unhappy that the explosives went to waste.

Suddenly, a tremor went through the water, causing clumps of sediment to fall off the wall and causing the rocks that composed it to clack together. It went on for fifteen seconds, stopping just before Bridget ordered the abortion of the dive.

"And that's our answer," Johnnie chirped.

"That's one answer, anyway. Still a few to find," Peters said. Bridget wondered how he could manage to sound dour through the tinny intercom.

They swam around the site, noting a small pile here, another there. One section formed a hollow square that looked like the foundations of a house.

"Guys, you need to see this." Johnnie sounded excited and very, very young.

They swam over and were confronted with what looked like a giant slab of stone, held in place by other stones wedged under it. The eroded edges seemed to indicate great age, but whatever rock it was made of had survived millennia with its gleaming white tone unscathed.

Another miniature tremor shook the water around them. Bridget thought they felt much more pleasant in the sea than on land, gentler somehow. This one went on for a few minutes, but she decided it wasn't any risk. How important could it be if the villagers were so unconcerned? But Peters was studying the ripples caused by the vibration. "I think this is the epicenter," he said after a while.

"How could you possibly know?"

"See how the waves in the silt on the sea floor here are clearly facing away from it? Now come over here and look at these. Also looking away. You'll find the same no matter where you go. This is the center of the tremors."

For some reason, that unsettled Bridget. They still had a good ten minutes left before they had to start their ascent, but she decided to cut it short. "We're going up, now. I want to discuss this with the whole team."

Greg's voice came through again, "What did you guys find?" But they ignored him again. He could look at the footage later.

"Peters, are you coming?"

"Just a minute. I'm having a last look."

It was more than a minute, but he eventually rose to their level, and they made their way back to the waiting ship. They climbed aboard and peeled off what they could and set sail towards the shore.

Ten minutes later, a small geyser shot out of the water behind them. Bridget turned to Peters.

"You didn't!"

His shrug was answer enough.

#

She'd ordered the captain to stop right there. They would have it out on the boat where the arrogant, pompous bastard wouldn't be able to go off to another room and ignore her.

"How could you do such a thing? We had solid proof of the Black Sea Deluge, probably the source of all the flood myths, from the Akkadian ones all the way to the Bible. We had the evidence we needed to lay to answer the oldest question in civilization and you blew it up? Are you a complete imbecile?"

"I set the charge so it wouldn't damage the walls. Don't worry."

"Then why—"

"I want to know what was under that slab. It just looked like some kind of lid to me. Maybe ancient gold, treasure, idols. Who knows? We can have a look tomorrow, and maybe we'll come out of this rich men and women."

"You aren't coming back tomorrow," Bridget said. "You're off the team."

Peters opened his mouth to respond, but whatever he said was drowned out by a roar that made the prior geyser sound like a stone thrown into a pond. An upwelling of water towered above their heads, splashing down onto the surface of the sea moments later. Huge waves sped towards their small ship.

The captain cursed and tried to point the nose of the craft into the oncoming wall of water, but they were pushed in reverse like a backward surfer for what seemed like an eternity. Some miracle kept the boat afloat and upright, but Bridget saw the second story of a house fly past to their right, followed by the top of a vendor's cart. Then she heard a crunch and was thrown backward into something unyielding.

Darkness.

#

"Are you all right? Bridget, can you hear me?" She opened her eyes to see Greg's face, paler than usual, only inches from her own. Not exactly the kind of thing a girl wanted to see first thing in the morning. She wondered how drunk she'd been the night before to allow this to happen.

And then her memory returned. "Oh, my God. What happened?" she asked.

"I think you need to see this." Greg held out his arm, and after a moment's hesitation as she allowed the world to stop spinning, Bridget took it. She could hear unidentified crashes and booms off in the background somewhere. As far as she could tell, she'd been lying on the deck of the boat. "Over there," he said.

She felt her mouth fall agape. Towering over the village's collection of one- and two-story buildings, a huge … thing … approached from the sea. The head looked feline, somehow, and scribed as if it were composed of tiny lines. The rest of the body looked human—or at least humanoid—but thicker and built to withstand the weight of a mound of flesh five floors high. It was covered with thick black bristles, but not thoroughly. Many morning papers would be running edited versions of the picture, since full frontal nudity on that scale would shock readers in quite a few nations.

"What is it?" she breathed.

Greg shrugged and looked down, a sign that he was going to show off. "I think it's Humbaba," he said.

Bridget was about to ask what a Humbaba was when her years of archaeology background silenced the question. She knew exactly who and what it was. "Humbaba is a myth, Greg. And how would you know what it was? I thought you were into computers, not ancient legends." Peters had probably told him, she thought.

He looked down again, shrugged. "Google-fu," he replied, showing her a search engine result on some kind of handheld device with an image of an ancient statue that, to be fair, looked a lot like the monster on a rampage in front of them.

She rolled her eyes. He would, when faced with a shipwreck, save his electronics and look stuff up before coming to her aid. "Where are Peters and Johnnie?"

"They went to see if they could be of any help. It was quite a wave, after all. Lots of dead Bulgarians."

Since the monster seemed otherwise preoccupied, she took a second to observe their surroundings. The fishing boat had wedged between two houses, and the impact had caused quite a bit of splintering along the wooden hull. She doubted it would ever be seaworthy again even if they ever got it out of the place it had jammed. "How do we get down?"

He led her to the prow which, due to the angle of the street was nearly level with the cobbles, and they climbed off. The stones were still wet, and an abandoned fish or two attempted to breathe with little success. The monster, though moving slowly, had reached the shoreline. Bridget could see that the writers of the old epic had gotten it precisely right: it did have the face of a lion, and its breath was, quite obviously, of flame. When it came to giant monsters, those ancient Sumerians clearly knew their stuff.

The monster had been silent, but now it was bellowing, sending a gout of flame out with each scream.

"Illameeeeees!" it shouted. "Illameeeeees!"

It was a wall of sound, painful to hear, and almost impossible to decipher. "What's it saying?" Greg's shouted question, after that aural assault, seemed like a whisper from across a meadow.

How could she know? Even if she spoke whatever language the creature was shouting in— ancient Akkadian?—how could he possibly expect her to make out words in that noise?

"Illameeeeees!"

She covered her ears, but the sound went straight through her hands. If not for the fact that it was five blocks away, she would have been deafened.

Suddenly, she knew what the monster was shouting.

"It's looking for Gilgamesh," she cried, despite the pain.

"What?" Greg was holding his head between his hands, obviously trying to block out the sound.

"Gilgamesh!"

"Yes, that's where the legend comes from," he replied.

"No, that's what the creature is shouting. Humbaba is looking for Gilgamesh." The ambient noise made it difficult to get the idea across, but eventually they managed to understand each other.

The knowledge didn't galvanize them into action. They might have been the only two people in the village who knew what was going on, but that didn't change the fact that they were just tiny humans, no match for a creature somehow returned from the age of legend. They watched helplessly as it walked through the village, reducing houses hundreds of years old to rubble in seconds.

All Bridget felt during the horror was thankfulness that the creature had chosen a path that would avoid them entirely, and thankfulness that the noise, which would have been incapacitating at that distance, were being sent in a different direction. The survival instinct warred with the voyeuristic: they hid, but they watched.

The culmination of Humbaba's rage occurred at the village church, an ancient stone structure on a hill slightly beyond the houses. The monster walked up to it, absently knocked over the slender steeple tower and attacked the roof.

"Illameeeeees!"

It shouted into the hole it had made in the slate tiles, and they later learned that the sound had killed half of the thirty people huddled inside and deafened the remainder. It seemed that ancient gods still had priority over newer ones.

Finally, Humbaba got its rage under control for a few moments. It stood, sniffed the wind, took its bearings, and headed off towards the southeast. Neither Greg nor Bridget moved until it was well out of sight. Then, Greg collapsed onto the floor and cried like a baby.

#

The next two days were unsettled.

Most of their luggage had been washed away by the wave, along with the proprietors of the small hotel in which they'd been staying. Other than Greg's handheld, their electronics were shot, and what clothes remained had to be washed in fresh water to remove the salt. Or at least that was what they thought before learning that the water, too, was out. Cell phone service was the only thing still working, but the Bulgarian government saw to that extremely quickly. A full shut-down of the area occurred while they investigated.

Bridget's team seemed to be the only group of people who'd come through relatively unscathed, apart from a nasty gash on Johnnie's forehead, which could have done with better medical attention than the amateur bandage applied by Peters. None was available.

The Bulgarian army arrived within hours of the catastrophe, and the group, as suspicious foreign scientists, were immediately detained. Everyone was polite and solicitous, but there was no question of their leaving, which made Peters furious. He'd wanted to take any of the cars lying around untended and leave the area before the authorities arrived. It seemed he had experience with unfortunate circumstances, something Bridget didn't remember seeing on his otherwise brilliant scientific résumé.

Essentially, they were punted into a room and told to avoid making a nuisance of themselves while the government decided what to do with them. A few hours later, some scared-looking soldiers, too young for the assault rifles they carried, installed a TV and switched it on. It showed three channels, two in Bulgarian and one in Russian. The Russian channel seemed to consist of a twenty-four-hour cycle of game shows and celebrity interviews, with some Big Brother thrown in to spice things up.

The Bulgarian channels were both locked into a twenty-four-hour news cycle. They seemed to be filming the monster as it walked across miles of farmland. The running commentary sounded tired, but the scientists watched the feed with interest.

"Where do you think it's going?" Greg asked.

"Bloody Lebanon, of course." Peters' reply just beat Bridget's, which made her angry. Angrier still that the man was right and had his Gilgamesh theory fresher than hers.

"Why?" This time, Johnnie chimed up, and she was happy to see him talking. He'd always been a bit shy, but after the incident he'd been nearly silent.

This time, she beat Peters to the punch. "Lebanon is where his ancient forest is thought to have been. That's where Utu, the god of the Sun in Mesopotamia set him to guard the trees. And that's where Gilgamesh is supposed to have betrayed him and killed him."

"Seems he didn't do much of a job of it, did he?" Peters observed dourly.

"Well, someone trapped him for thousands of years. Maybe Gilgamesh did kill him, and they buried him there but he revived."

"I doubt it. If the monster had been dead, why create that impenetrable lid for his tomb?" He paused. "And why flood hundreds of thousands of square kilometers of perfectly good farmland to keep him down there?"

Bridget was shocked. "You think ... You think people caused the Black Sea deluge, the biblical flood? That's impossible."

"Yes, just like building the pyramids was impossible." He looked her in the eye. "Maybe aliens did it."

"But ..." He was right. Even primitive people had basic tools. Even a thousand years ago, people could dig large holes in the ground. It would have taken years, but the passage to the Mediterranean could have been enlarged and deepened by the ancients. It would have been a question of keeping the slaves in line and not minding a death or two.

The day dragged by as the monster did nothing but walk.

#

A colonel in the Bulgarian army came around the next day. He told them that the British Embassy would be sending someone round to pick them up, but that the government still wanted their help with the inquest, so they would look at it as a boon if they stayed in Bulgaria for a while.

Peters straightened and gave the military man a hard look. "Why are you letting us go?"

"You are citizens of the European Union," he replied. "You are free to come and go as you choose."

"I'm not," Greg said.

"You are American," the colonel replied. Greg looked puzzled at this, but the Europeans knew exactly what he meant: it was easier to release the guy than to deal with the prissy letters of protest.

Peters was unconvinced. "What's the real reason?"

The colonel hesitated but then smiled and nodded his respect. "It's no secret. In an hour or two, the creature is scheduled to cross the border, at which time this is no longer a Bulgarian problem. Let the Turks deal with it." He turned and left.

The Turks tried to deal with it. They had a tank division—Peters informed them as to what a division was—waiting at the border, along with air support. As soon as Humbaba set foot in their territory, tearing down a large, sturdy border fence as he did, they opened fire.

The ancient creature ignored them, except for one tank that it picked up like a toy and tossed into the distance. It swatted absently at the fighters, but none flew near enough to grab.

"Oh, my God," Peters said. His normally inexpressive face had turned ashen.

"What now?" Johnnie asked.

"Now we find out if the Turks have nukes," the older man replied.

"What? Why?" Bridget heard herself ask. Heard herself shriek was more like it.

"Think about it. The only way to cross the water onto Asia is—"

"Through Istanbul!" Greg crowed triumphantly, like a small child able to follow the logic of its elders. And then his face fell. "Oh."

"Precisely. Can you imagine the damage that thing would do to a city of millions? Just its screams would cause a humanitarian catastrophe worse than the Southeast Asian Tsunami. The Turks must stop it if they can, any way they can. They don't have a choice."

They didn't get to see what the Turks tried next because the man from the British embassy herded them into two Land Rovers with the letters UN stenciled onto the sides.

Three hours later, they were in Sofia, all of them denying any knowledge of where the creature might have come from other than to say that they'd seen it rise about a mile offshore. The ruins would be there for anyone who bothered to look, and they saw no need to become accessories to whatever happened next.

All mention of explosives was suspended until later that evening. The group was watching TV— CNN had live coverage of what they were predictably calling The Creature from the Black Sea —and were all relieved that the Turks had decided to forego the nuclear option and were evacuating Istanbul instead.

"You knew, didn't you?" Bridget asked Peters, point blank.

He looked surprised but nodded. Then he put his finger to his lips, pointed to random places on the walls and pantomimed unseen listeners with headphones. Bridget wondered again who he really was. All the man said was, "I think every archaeologist in the world suspected that there was a tomb lost in the Black Sea somewhere. Most of them thought it was a temple, more symbol than reality. I guess this just proves them wrong."

She wanted to remind him that he'd signed up as a marine biologist, not an archaeologist, but stayed silent. He would probably shut up like a clam if she made an issue of that. "So how do we stop it?"

"Why would we want to stop him? Humbaba will just go into Lebanon and let the trees grow. That's what he does. Although it will probably do the terrorists a bit of no good, which they deserve, too. Why would we want to stop it?"

*Because I feel responsible*, Bridget thought. *I was the one who funded your little expedition. It's my fault that thing is out there, killing people with its screams. The old woman who ran the hotel, the people in that church.* She said, "I just think that, since we were there at the beginning, we should try to help it end," she said. Peters' grey eyes looked into hers. He swore. He knew what was being left unsaid.

"I suppose we'd need Gilgamesh."

Bridget tsked in irritation. "Gilgamesh is a myth. Please take this seriously."

Peters just looked at her, and she felt silly. "But Gilgamesh is dead," she amended lamely.

"Are you using the same source material that told us that Humbaba was dead?" She didn't reply. "Good, then we can assume that if Humbaba is still up and running, then the guy who bested him—even if he didn't slay him, but lured him into a pit and then covered him with a very large rock held in place by tons of water pressure—is still out there somewhere?"

"I guess. So where is he?"

He gave her another steely gaze, and Greg and Johnnie, silent witnesses, were completely forgotten. "Do you really want to do this? By all accounts, Gilgamesh is a pretty nasty guy. I'm half convinced that Humbaba is still mad at humanity because our little human hero betrayed him in the first place."

She hesitated. Some things were so enormous that you had to stop to think about it. But some guilt was so heavy that it gave you no choice. "Yes, this has to end. Where is he?"

"Well," Peters began, "You need to understand that this theory has been dismissed, ridiculed even, by all respectable archaeologists …"

She listened, spellbound, knowing her orderly scientific life was something lost in the past. Or overtaken by the past. Or something.

But it was definitely gone.

# 15 SURVEYING SAVIORS

## H.L. Pauff

"We are within range," Kutyl said. "It is appearing on the viewing monitors now."

Kritef and Kutyl watched as the planet came into focus on the monitor. A shroud of dark satellites swirled over the planet, obscuring its true nature. "I have never seen a global weather system quite like this. The instruments indicate that there is an incredible amount of precipitation," Kritef said. He tried a few different settings on his panel, hoping his instruments could pierce the clouds so that they could see the surface, but a combination of the clouds' thickness and interference from severe lightning storms were stopping him. "Have you ever seen such a thing?"

"I have not personally seen a phenomenon like this," Kutyl said. "However, I have read files in the archives that described similar events. The surveyors that came across them were unable to provide a sufficient explanation. It defies science."

"I suppose, then, that this planet warrants further exploration? How much time shall we allocate to this planet? Remember, there are a few moons in this system orbiting their gaseous giants that might be of interest. I am anxious to investigate all of them."

Kutyl surveyed his instruments, looking for any blips on the planet's surface. "Let us descend and make a quick sweep. If there is nothing of interest other than the weather, then we shall hurry to explore the rest of the system before we are due back." Kutyl took control of their craft from the artificial intelligence and gently brought the ship into the atmosphere. Huge raindrops pelted their viewing screens and heavy winds rocked them. Streaks of jagged red lightning lit up the sky.

Inside the atmosphere, their instruments were able to scan the planet looking for anything of note. They calibrated specifically for rare minerals and other resources, but they also detected anomalous-like life forms.

"I see nothing but liquid. No apparent landmasses," Kutyl said, studying the viewing screens. "Sensors indicate that this planet's atmosphere is comprised of a mixture that you and I would find agreeable, if we desired to step out of our ship."

Kritef looked at the endless stretch of water and the dark clouds with their heavy rains that continued to feed it. "I think it prudent that we remain inside. I do not understand how it could be raining everywhere simultaneously. Truly bizarre. Is there anything else of note here?" Kritef asked.

Kutyl checked the results of the ship's scanning instruments. "Yes. I detect lots of debris in the water. An incredible amount, really. I suspect that these rains and apparent global flood have destroyed some form of civilization. Also, we are picking up some small landmasses that are still above water. Let us investigate.

Kutyl directed the ship towards a tiny chain of islands that looked ready to succumb to the heavy rains at any moment.

"There are individuals down there," Kutyl said. "Huddled around fires, wearing clothing and working with tools."

Kritef sat up, his interest piqued. "Intelligence? Let us bring them aboard."

"I do not believe that to be wise," Kutyl said. "The objective of our expedition is to survey, not to interfere."

"Correct, but are we not also held to a code of ethics? If these beings are truly intelligent, is it not our duty to aid them in their greatest time of need? Look at the state of this world. Water has overrun everything, and it continues to rain. They will not survive long."

Kutyl scrunched his face at his partner. "Should we not let things proceed naturally? Perhaps this world is like this because of their own design? We have seen plenty of evidence that most civilizations are not viable long-term."

"Nonsense. Let us bring them aboard and meet them personally. Look at them. They scarcely have even the most rudimentary of tools. This is not their fault. It could not be. These are just beings that wish to live and prosper, like all beings."

Kutyl relented and allowed Kritef to bring the beings aboard the ship. The beings screamed as their pink fleshy limbs flailed, and they floated through the air into the belly of the silver craft hovering in the air. The surveyors visited a few more island chains spread out across the planet and found even more survivors they promptly brought on board.

When their holding chamber was near max capacity, the two surveyors came down to the chamber and looked upon their guests through a one-way window.

"They look tired yet so full of life," Kritef said.

Kutyl rolled his eyes. "I can smell them even through these thick walls."

Kritef chuckled and clasped his friend's shoulder. "Just think. These are beings that have survived the most calamitous of events that have drowned their world. They are hardy and strong, the best their species has to offer. Wherever we settle them, I know they will go on to great things. Perhaps, if time permits, we can return for more of them."

The beings wandered around the chamber screaming, punching, and kicking at the walls. The surveyors had to wait until their computers could acclimate to their language and allow the two different species to communicate.

"Greetings," Kritef said through an intercom. The action in the chamber stopped and all the beings looked to the ceiling. They cowered in fear from the deep, disembodied voice of Kritef.

"Do not be afraid," he told them. "We are visitors from another world." With the pressing of a button, the window became translucent, and the two species could see each other. The two surveyors could hear the gasps from the pink fleshy beings. "We see your world at the end of its life, and we are here to help. There may be no future for your drowned world, but there will be a future for you and as many more of your species as we can rescue. We will find you a new world where you can prosper. In the meantime, you are our guests for the foreseeable future. You will eat our food and drink our drinks and make our ship your new home. A number of automatons roam the side of the ship you are on and will help you where they can. Do not be afraid of them."

A few doors in the chamber opened and the beings immediately ran to them. The doors lead to other parts of the ship: the dining areas, the bathing areas, and the recreation areas. The beings would not be able to access the part of the ship where Kritef and Kutyl resided, but they would have everything they needed.

"They are not so bad. Would you concede that?" Kritef asked his partner.

"They appear harmless enough," Kutyl said.

The surveyors finished their review of the water world and found many civilizations had been buried beneath the flood. An untold number of this world's inhabitants had perished in this great event and the two surveyors felt a sense of pride that they were able to save some of them.

It only took the journey to the system's fifth planet for the beings to become comfortable in the ship. They began to explore, allowing themselves to sample the food and drink. When enough of them had tried and were convinced that it was not poisoned, a celebration broke out.

They cheered their redemption from certain doom and sang songs about a glorious new era to come. The celebration continued throughout Kritef's and Kutyl's sleep cycles and well into the next day until one by one the beings collapsed from exhaustion.

"They sure know how to celebrate," Kutyl said. "My sleep cycle was insufficient. I hope this does not continue."

"They have been delivered from their deaths. I believe their celebrating is appropriate."

Kutyl and Kritef surveyed the gas giant and its many moons looking for anything of significance. There were several interesting geological formations and some evidence that the moons could one day support conditions that could harbor life, but none of it was as interesting as the beings that roamed the ship.

One of their kind rose from its slumber and awakened the others. A few of the beings took the food and stored it in sealed buckets in some of the warmer rooms in the hope that it would ferment and produce a special type of drink that they all craved. The men ran rampant, destroying crucial parts of the ship and leaving their bodily waste wherever they chose. There were arguments over food and arguments over who would be allowed to copulate with the females of their species. Fights began to break out across the ship over the smallest of things, including misunderstandings and accidental

76

bumps. The automatons attempted to get the situation under control, but they were overpowered, destroyed, and in some cases subjected to copulation.

Even the women, who the two surveyors believe to be the more sophisticated of the species, wreaked havoc. They ran gambling operations and recruited men to fight for their entertainment. By the time Kutyl's and Kritef's sleep cycles neared, the ship was almost in ruins.

"They are uncivilized monsters," Kutyl said. "We must return them to their planet of origin. Their world was drowned because of the very evidence we see with our own eyes. Surely, they have brought upon their own doom."

Kritef watched the viewing monitors with disgust but did not agree. "We do not know their customs. This could very well be a part of a ritual of celebration. It could be many cycles before they are finished celebrating and can continue with their lives. Perhaps whatever deities they worship demand this of them. Would you be so cruel as to return them to their deaths? Where is your patience?"

Kutyl sat back in his chair and grunted. "If we exhibit any more patience, we might not have a ship at all."

By the time they reached the last planet in the system, even Kritef could not believe what he was witnessing. "Surely, they have no more cause to celebrate?" The beings had destroyed most of their section of the ship. They tore down walls and rolled in their own excrement, refusing to make use of the widely available cleansing apparatuses.

A clear division of factions began to emerge with the physically strongest banding together to terrorize the weak. Even with ample resources of food and water available for them, the factions began to fight unnecessarily over the resources, and it did not take long for blood to mar the hallways.

"Why do they simply not share and enjoy? Why must they fight and kill and take from each other? I do not understand this behavior," Kutyl said. "There are so few of them, one would think they would band together to persevere. If we present these beings as the triumph of our expeditions to the Galactic Council or even to our own superiors, we will be stripped of our ranks and titles."

"I will address them," Kritef said. He stood and took a step towards the door that would lead him to the observation room overlooking the chamber.

Kutyl placed a hand on Kritef's shoulder and stopped him. "Do not address them," he said. "I fear your mere presence will whip them into an even greater frenzy. Before long, they could break down the barriers between us and attempt to copulate with *you*."

Kritef hated to admit when he misjudged a situation, especially to Kutyl. "Perhaps you are correct." He sighed. "I fear what would happen if we settle these people on another world. I fear that they would treat it as they currently treat our ship. I fear that that world would end up like their current world. These beings are out of control and have no limits. Surely, wherever they go, a drowned world is sure to follow. We must return them at once in a hurry. We are beyond late in returning to our own system."

Kutyl and Kritef pressed their ship to travel as fast as possible. Upon arrival at the third planet, they found that the dark clouds covering the entire world had disappeared and the water had begun to recede. Gigantic arcs of colorful rainbows soared over all the visible landmasses.

"It is as if we are viewing an entirely different planet," Kritef said.

"It is the same," Kutyl said. "Let us descend and return them."

They entered the planet's atmosphere and scanned the landmasses for a suitable drop spot. All around the planet, on every landmass, they found beings that looked much like the ones their ship held. These beings were singing and dancing with joy, but they were not reckless like the guests on the ship. They were not stealing and gambling and shedding blood. They were sharing and exhibiting kindness. They aided each other as they attempted to piece their destroyed lives back together.

"Surely, these are the people we would have preferred to welcome aboard our ship," Kritef said. "They have survived a cataclysmic event. They are stronger for it and appear to have preferable temperaments to the survivors we have picked up."

"Yes. Let us hope that the wicked have all gone with the water and that only the pure remain."

"If that is the case, then we cannot reintroduce these wicked beings back to this planet," Kritef said. "That would not be right."

"Well, we certainly cannot keep them on board nor take them anywhere with us. The supplies we had that were supposed to last thousands of cycles will barely last another handful. We must return them if you and I are to survive."

"It is a shame," Kritef said. "I can always place them in the middle of a body of water." He looked at Kutyl who shook his head and began to talk of the code of ethics before Kritef stopped him. Kritef sighed and hovered over the instrument panel, directing the ship to place the survivors in a small village.

The villagers were in the middle of placing thatched roofs atop their newly constructed homes and were shocked when several unfamiliar beings of their own kind materialized amongst them.

Kutyl lifted the ship out of the atmosphere and headed towards the deep blackness of space, but Kritef kept their viewing instruments trained on the village. He watched as the new arrivals began to assault the peaceful people trying to rebuild.

"I fear we have destroyed this world a second time," Kritef said.

# 16 THE SHARPTOOTH

## Terry Alexander

"Thomas, help me. I lost my footing." The old man's panicked scream rose above the storm's tumult. Thunder rumbled through the slate gray sky, and the air tingled for a moment as lightning split the sky.

"Keep moving," Thomas shouted. He pushed several stragglers forward. "We have to keep moving if we hope to survive."

"If the rain doesn't stop soon, even this high ground won't be safe." Rachael, a young woman carrying a swaddling child, glared at the bearded man. "We haven't had any rest in two days. We need sleep, and food."

"Our survival is there." Thomas pointed at the cloud-covered peaks. "If you hope to survive, keep moving." He dropped to the rear of the line. A gray-haired man gripped a small tree as the water swirled around him. The man's head disappeared beneath the fierce undertow.

"Thomas, help me, please." The gray-haired man spit out a mouthful of water. "The bottom feeders are nibbling on my toes. Hurry, while there's time. The Sharptooth will be here soon."

Thomas licked his lips. He placed one foot in the cold, swirling water. A small fish darted around his ankles, nibbling at his flesh. He forced his way through the current. Something beneath the dark water clutched at the hem of his garment, pulling him down.

He felt blindly under the water for his attacker. A large fish had snapped a loose strand of his robe and pulled him under. Thomas pried its jaws from the coarse cloth and fought his way to the surface. He coughed, hacking water from his lungs. A thick mucus ran from his nostrils. The water had risen two feet during the short time he attempted to rescue the old man.

"Thomas," The man screamed. "I want to live, one more day, one more hour. I want to live."

"I can't help you. I'm sorry." Raindrops pelted Thomas's face and streamed down his cheeks. "I can't get to you, Barnabas."

Barnabas reached up, catching hold of a higher branch. "You're going to leave me here to die? Why me? Why not Rachael and her brat, or Stephen? They are no better than me."

"We may all die," Thomas said, wiping his eyes. "None of us may live to see tomorrow. We must keep climbing to have any hope at all."

Two long, meaty tentacles sprang from the water. The sharp tips of the tentacles impaled Barnabas, ripping through his flesh and protruding through his back. The color drained from his face as blood ran down the tentacle into the rushing maelstrom. "The Sharp—" Barnabas's body trembled as the tentacles dragged him under the water.

Thomas reached for the old man's outstretched hand. Water swirled around his thighs before he realized the futility of trying to save the old man. A massive body broke through the surface. Long, flexible tentacles lifted Barnabas above the beast's gaping mouth. A large, soulless eye peered at Thomas. An icy lump formed in the pit of his stomach and tingled up his spine.

*Was that a smile?* Thomas pondered. He took a step back, desperate to get out of the rising water. *That was a smile, I know it was.* He stood transfixed, his legs unwilling to move, staring at the creature he knew only from legend.

The mouth opened wide, the tentacles moving Barnabas closer to the daggers of sharp teeth. "No," Barnabas moaned. He freed his right arm and braced it against the creature's open mouth. His arm slipped on the slick skin and disappeared into the mouth. Sharp, ragged teeth fastened themselves onto flesh, tearing the old man's arm from his body.

Blood squirted from the old man's shoulder, painting the monster in garish crimson. Barnabas screamed. He struck the creature with his remaining hand, over and over, the blows progressively getting weaker. The struggle snapped Thomas from his trance, he ran to catch up with the others in his group.

"You have to move faster." He caught Rachael easily and got a glimpse of the next refugee in line fifty feet ahead. "Come on, faster. Pick up the pace. The water is rising faster now."

"I can't, Thomas. I can't keep up." Tears mixed with the rain on Rachael's face. "My feet and legs are blistered. I can't do it anymore."

"Give Horace to me. I'll carry him. That'll lessen your load and you can catch up with the others." Thomas reached for the baby.

"He died this morning. I haven't produced milk since yesterday. My husband said I was past my prime when I became pregnant. I thought I could handle a new child at my age. I was wrong." Rachael licked her lips. "I wanted to find a place to bury him. Someplace where the water won't carry him away."

"Why didn't you tell me? I could have had one of the other women help."

"Share her milk with my child and risk not having enough for her own? I wouldn't do it, and I wouldn't ask anyone to do it for me." She sat on a large rock. "I'm going to sit here and let the water take me."

"No, we've got to keep moving. The Sharptooth killed Barnabas." Thomas grabbed Rachael's arm and pulled her forward.

"I'm not going." She pulled away and stamped her feet in the mud, sinking past her ankles. Her gray-streaked hair lay flat and lifeless on her head as she brushed the bangs from her forehead. "I saw a sharptooth when I was a child. I've always wanted to see one again."

"Rachael, it'll devour you." Thomas watched the floodwaters rise behind Rachael. "We have to keep moving."

"My child and I aren't going to survive." She closed her eyes. "If you are going to lead these people to safety, you need to move on."

"Please, Rachael, come with me."

"Go on, Thomas, while you still have time." She returned to the large stone, closed her eyes, and hummed. It took Thomas a second to realize she was humming a lullaby. He slogged his way up the steep incline. Several minutes later, he passed a man lying on the side of the path. He couldn't place the man's name. The man had slipped on the rocks and fell to the hard unyielding stones. A bloody bone protruded through the skin of his lower leg.

"Thomas, please help me. I can make it. I know I can." The man begged. "Just help me to my feet."

"It's over for you," Thomas said, evading the man's clutching hands. "Use your dagger. Open a vein and bleed out. It's better than being eaten by The Sharptooth."

"Don't believe in monsters." The man shook his head, water drops flying from the ends of his hair. His hands clutched at the stones and grass as he pulled himself toward Thomas. "They're nothing but stories parents tell their children to keep them in line."

"Barnabas was eaten by one." Thomas said. "Take the easy way out. Slit your wrist and make it deep." He hurried up the trail.

"You're a coward, Thomas. You have no spine." The man's words burned in Thomas's ears, taunting him.

A rickety rope bridge stretched over a gorge ahead. The flood water lapped at the bottom of the worn boards. The bulk of his group rushed across the flimsy boards. *What are they doing?* Thomas ran forward, waving his arms above his head. "Stop, come back. That bridge isn't safe."

"Save your breath. They know the bridge is in bad shape. It's the quickest way to the summit." Loretta stepped from around a mound of large stones. The rain pelted her face as she moved away from the makeshift shelter. "They know the risks."

"The planks are worn and rotten. They'll never make it across." Thomas stared into Loretta's eyes. "Why didn't you go with them?"

"I'm nearly blind. My presence there would endanger the group. I chose to stay behind." Her milky eyes returned Thomas's intense stare. "They tied ropes around their waists, so they're all connected in a long line. It was Terrell's idea. If one person falls, the two closest will come to their aid."

"We can make it to the upper trail. It's a safer trail to the peak." Thomas ran forward, waving his arms. No one on the bridge acknowledged he was there.

"Come back," he shouted. "The upper trail is clear. We can reach the summit."

"What's that?" Loretta grabbed his arm from behind. "Something's in the water. It's huge. Can you make it out?"

"It's trees." Thomas ran to the edge of the chasm. "They washed out and the current stacked them together." He waved his arms. "Hurry, run!"

"Run." Loretta screamed. "That snag will tear the bridge out." She pointed frantically at the solid mass closing on the rope structure.

A young man at the rear of the line noticed the trees. He hurried forward, urging the woman in front of him to move faster. She saw the danger and ran to the next man in line. Within seconds, the entire line pushed toward the far side of the divide.

A board snapped, then another, and several more gave way. A man and woman fell through, the swift moving current tugging at them. Several people grabbed the rope, pulling them toward the gap. More planks snapped under a burly man. His feet splashed in the swirling water. A thin woman standing behind him caught the collar of his garment and held on.

"Hurry," Thomas shouted. "Get to the other side. Hurry!"

A huge root-ball snagged in the ropes, yanking the bridge forward. Several people disappeared under the snag. Others were yanked off their feet, clinging to the rough bark. The forward momentum stopped momentarily with the ropes stretched to their limits.

The wooden planks snapped. Ropes groaned under the strain as the tremendous weight of the snag pushed forward. The first rope popped, followed quickly by the second. Within the span of a single breath the huge snag tore away and floated out toward open water.

"Thomas, help us." A sad, forlorn voice came from the snag.

Thomas and Loretta stared in silence as the makeshift island floated away. "We've got to reach the upper trail. If we reach the summit, we'll be safe." Thomas grabbed her hand and gave it a squeeze. "Come on. We can't waste any more time."

"You should leave me. I'll slow you down."

"Someone has to live." Thomas pulled Loretta forward. "Someone has to survive."

"I thought Noah was insane when he built that monstrosity." A mirthless chuckle passed her lips. "Then they gathered a male and female of all the land animals, and the entire village laughed at him."

"I remember. How everyone chuckled when the rain started." Thomas steered her to a well-worn path through the stones. "The water lapping at the side of that huge barge. It shouldn't have floated so easily."

Loretta squinted, staring into the distance. "What is that?"

"Elephant carcass. The current is carrying it to deeper water." His stomach growled. "If it were closer, I'd cut a chunk of hindquarter away."

"Can your knife cut elephant skin?"

Thomas struggled to maintain his footing. He reached and grabbed a nearby rock. "We must keep going. If we get to the highest place we can find, we'll survive."

"I love your optimism." She sank past her ankles in a patch of mud. "You didn't answer my question. Can your knife cut elephant skin?"

Thomas regained his footing and pulled Loretta free of the mud. "I have the sharpest dagger in all the land. It can cut anything."

"Men are all braggarts." Loretta nodded.

"We have to get far ahead of the rising water." Thomas squeezed her hand, encouraging her to keep moving. "I think the rain is breaking up to the north."

"Don't lie to me." She palmed rain from her forehead. "It's not going to stop raining. We're just delaying the inevitable. We're going to die."

"We can't give up. We must keep moving."

"Where is the flood water?"

"We've gained a lot of ground. We're at least a mile ahead of it now." He pulled her to a stop.

"What is it?"

"The snag is caught on the rocks ahead. The elephant has washed up on the trees. There's a horse there too."

Loretta squinted. "It's all a blob to me."

He slogged forward. "If we hurry, we can get some horse meat before the snag gets carried over the rocks."

"No." She shook her head. "That's a bad idea. Didn't you see The Sharptooth earlier? If we go down there, we'll die. Better to try for the summit."

"Okay, come on." They plodded forward, through sticky mud, over slick rocks.

After several hours, Loretta pulled away from Thomas's grip. "I can't go anymore. I've got to rest." She leaned against a massive rock.

"Rest. I'll check on ahead," Thomas said, trying to sound encouraging. "We must be close. I'll be back in a few minutes."

"I'm not going anywhere."

The trail grew steeper and the footing more treacherous. Thomas pulled himself forward using rocks embedded in the mud. His muscles quivered under the strain. Within minutes he found the summit. He collapsed to the soaked earth and looked around. He'd gained precious little on the advancing water.

"The barge, Noah's barge." He saw the huge ship bobbing on the surface nearly a mile away. "There it is." He drew in a deep breath and wiped the rain from his eyes. "If only we had a raft." He stared at his mud-covered feet and the hem of his filthy robe. "A raft."

The idea slapped him in the face. They had a raft. Thomas struggled to his feet and eased down the incline. On three occasions his feet slipped out from under him. Only his quick reflexes saved him from injury.

He spied Loretta. She leaned against the huge boulder near the path. "Loretta, I have a plan," he shouted. "We can survive. We can."

She didn't acknowledge his words.

"Loretta, we must get back to the snag. We can use it like a raft. We can live." He drew closer, staring at the silent woman. Her eyes closed, chin resting on her face. *Asleep, she's asleep.* Thomas reached out and touched her shoulder.

Loretta's body turned away from his touch and crashed to the ground.

"Wake up." He knelt beside her and turned her over. "Come on Loretta, wake up." His shaking grew more forceful. "Damn it, please wake up."

He held her for several minutes, slowly accepting his role as sole survivor. Thomas placed Loretta gently on the ground and folded her hands across her chest. "I've got to go, Loretta. I've got to get to the snag before it floats over the rocks."

He splashed down the trail, forcing his tired legs to an unsafe speed over the slick rocks and shifting mud. Within minutes he reached the spot. The rain had lifted the mass and weakened the stone's grip. Thomas placed his feet carefully on the steep slope. He hoped to negotiate his way to the snag.

With a snap of timbers, it lifted from the restraining stones. The current snatched it from the bank toward swifter water. Throwing caution to the wind, Thomas ran down the incline. His feet slid out from under him, and he hit the ground hard, sliding down the steep grade. He splashed into the water as the snag fell from his grasp.

"No!" Thomas shouted. "I won't die today. I won't." The current caught his body, pulling him under the waves. His hand closed on a large root. Fighting the swift water, he pulled himself onto the snag. He fell to his knees, coughing up water.

"Who's there?" A female voice shouted. "Answer me. Who's there?"

"Bridget, Bridget. It's Thomas. Where are you?"

"Thomas, is it really you?" Her voice gained strength. "I'm caught, the rope is wrapped around the tree trunks and holding me out of the water."

"You've got to talk louder. I can barely hear you." A massive clap of thunder shook the air. Lightning flashed to the water's surface, leaving a sulfurous odor.

"Bridget. Bridget, answer me." The intense drumming of the rain drowned out Thomas's words. He slipped and dropped to the slick bark, scrambling to keep from sliding into the water. He spied a short length of rope tangles in the tree branches. His hands closed on the braided hemp. Dragging himself across the knotty surface, Thomas followed the rope until it disappeared into a tangle of interlocked branches.

He stuck his head and upper torso into a tiny opening. "Bridget, can you move?"

"Thomas, it's good to see you." She forced a smile. "I can move one arm, and my head."

"I'll cut the rope and help you out of that mess."

"The only thing holding me above the water is the rope. My right leg is wedged between two trees. I can't get it free. If you cut the rope, I'll drown before you can get me out of this."

"Did anyone else survive?"

"I don't think so. Peter's about three feet from me. Most of his head is gone." She grew silent for nearly a minute. "Do you have any food? I'm so hungry."

"We have a dead horse and an elephant caught in the branches."

"How are you going to cook in this downpour?"

"We'll have to eat it raw."

"Cut me a small piece. I must eat something."

"Give me a minute." Thomas rose to his feet. The steady beat of the rain diminished as he made his way to the horse. Several sharp tree branches pierced the animal's hide. The body bobbed in the water just out of his reach. The small root-ball tipped behind him. Thomas edged forward, balancing himself on the slick bark.

He pulled the knife from his waist scabbard and sawed at the thick hide. The meat felt soft and spongy between his fingers. Small bits dropped into the swift current. He cut a long thick strip away. He turned and placed it behind. His hand closed on the hind leg. A slick round head split the water. Barbed tentacles shot forward and pierced the horse's lifeless body. The branches snapped, the thick sucker-covered arms ripped the body free and lifted it in the air. Stained water drained from the holes in the horse's body, flowing past the mouthful of sharp teeth to disappear into the dark void of a mouth. The shiny daggers of death snapped on the body and cleaved it in half in a single bite.

Thomas dropped to his back, his heart pounding in his chest. The dagger slipped from his slick fingers and tumbled into the water. His trembling hands closed on the strip of meat as he crawled to Bridget's nesting spot.

"The Sharptooth," he shouted. "It devoured the horse in a single gulp." The snag shook, each tree trembled and quivered. "Bridget, are you okay?"

No answer.

Thomas wiped the rain from his face and crawled into the hole. A raw bloody mess hung from the rope. Bridget's head and arm were missing. Blood dripped from her torn flesh. Bile churned his stomach and singed his throat. Vomit spewed past his lips and discolored the water for a brief instant. His nose burned as tears filled his eyes. He blinked them away long enough to spy the knife at Bridget's waist.

Thomas hooked his legs in the branches and reached for the blade. Stretching, his fingers grazed the handle. Readjusting his weight, he reached again and managed to pull the knife from Bridget's belt. Water rushed over his head.

A dark shape came up from the depths. A chill of dread seized his heart and squeezed as the mouth opened, displaying sharp, pointed teeth. In desperation, Thomas sought to find something to grip. His hand fastened on a tree branch. He pulled himself from the water, trying to squirm out of the hole. The head grew closer, a black eye focused on Thomas.

The head broke the surface and closed on Bridget's remains as Thomas rolled from the opening. He lay on the uneven surface, his arm draped across his eyes. *When will it end? When will this cursed rain end?*

Thomas wiped moisture from his eyes. Sitting up, he wrapped his arms around his knees. He glanced across the endless expanse of water. He imagined he saw the outline of the massive barge in the distance. He found a small bit of horsemeat. A foul odor filled his nostrils as he bit into the coarse grain and began to chew.

The makeshift raft shook violently. A set of tentacles gripped the branches along the edge of the snag. A massive head lifted from the water, its single eye focused on Thomas.

*I can't move. I've got to stay perfectly still. It'll kill me if I move.* His eyes locked on the monster. He scarcely felt the burn as the hooked tentacle plunged through his belly. A single scream burst from his lips as the creature lifted him toward its gaping mouth.

# OMEGA

# 17 ANGELBLOOD

## Frank Sawielijew

With feathers white as a cloud, on wings as pure as an angel's, the bird rose into the sky as close to God as was possible for a creature of the earth. White and pure, a flawless being representing the perfection of God's creation. Jabez smiled as he watched it disappear among the clouds.

"Rat of the skies, they call it. And what has it become now? Did you see, my dear Judith? Did you see what has become of it?" he asked his lover, his beloved, his wife.

"Yes, my love. I saw," she replied, gazing in awe. "I saw."

He put an arm around her, his smile growing wider. His heart felt as if it wished to jump out of his chest and dance on the ground—nay, through the sky in celebration. All the doubts, all the fears, all the arguments with his beloved were forgotten. The efforts of the past few months had not been in vain. It had worked.

It had worked.

"I'm sorry I ever doubted you, Jabez. I'm so sorry I ever—" Judith started, but Jabez sealed her lips with a kiss before she could continue.

"Forget it, my love," he said after his lips had left hers. "It doesn't matter. We succeeded. Do you know what this means? For our future, for our lives?"

She smiled, a smile as broad and full of mirth as his. "Yes. We could be kings."

He placed another kiss upon her lips. "No. Not kings. We shall be gods."

#

Arishat did not shield her face as she was assaulted with rotten fruits, nor did she lower her head in shame when hypocrite mouths flung accusations of sin at her. *Unclean*, they shouted, *sinful, filthy, rotten*.

*Whore.*

They loved to display their righteousness in public, but they were not without sin themselves. Some of them she knew. There was Ezekiel, who loved nothing more than to be pleasured by her mouth. Hafet, who had a wife and three children but spent more time with Arishat than with his family. Jeremiah, who paid her extra if she treated him like a dog.

Now, out on the street, they called her whore. At night, when the city slept, they came to her in secret and paid in silver to live out the sinful fantasies they were too afraid to admit to their wives. Only a few faces in the crowd gave her looks of sympathy. She knew them, too. Isaiah, who had lost his wife to disease and found solace in Arishat's arms at night. Poor Argurios, who was shunned by the people of this city for worshipping different gods.

Just like Arishat herself.

"Get out of here, you worthless mutt!" she heard a voice shout from within a nearby house, followed by the whimpering of a hungry dog.

A sad little creature crawled through the door, its fur dirty and matted. As soon as it spotted Arishat, the dog's spirits lifted, and it approached her with a wagging tail.

"Kalbat, my little girl!" said Arishat as she knelt to pat its head. "You're hungry, aren't you? And none of these people have any food to spare for a stray like you. They treat you like garbage, you poor thing."

This was how stray dogs were treated around here. No wonder Jeremiah always told her to treat him like a dog when he wanted to be whipped and degraded.

"Look at this, the bitch and the whore are best friends! What a charming little pair!" yelled a voice from the crowd. The cruel joke was met with roaring laughter.

"Come, Kalbat. Let's go to Uncle Noah. Maybe he has some scraps for you."

Arishat got up and followed the street to the city gate. Kalbat followed close on her heels. Occasionally, a mushy piece of fruit would hit her, followed by a deriding comment. Most people ignored her now, as they'd had their entertainment for the day. The whore had been made fun of, and business on the streets could continue as usual.

This city had been her home for more than five years now. Arishat had long gotten used to this treatment.

#

Noah's house was not far from the city walls. The old man preferred the peace of the countryside to the hubbub of city life, and his new project required a lot of space to be built, too. It was almost finished, and it looked impressive.

"Arishat! It's nice to see you again!" Noah called as he spotted her standing in the fields. When he noticed that she didn't turn around to greet him because her eyes were still taking in the sight of the ship, he asked, "Do you like it?"

"It's impressive," she said. "My people know a lot about building boats, but this … it's something else."

Noah had been told by God to build a great ship with enough space to house all the creatures of God's creation. It stretched higher than any house Arishat had ever seen. She wondered how many trees had to be felled to get so much wood. It looked like an entire forest had been sacrificed to build this boat.

"Yes. God showed me how to build it. I think I did a pretty good job." A jovial smile formed on Noah's lips. "With this, I'm pretty sure we'll survive the flood."

Arishat shook her head. "I still don't get it. Why would your god do this? I know he's a vengeful god, but you are his chosen people. He can't just kill you all!"

"Well, not all of us."

"But almost. If your family is the only one to survive, how will you carry on your legacy? You will be swallowed by larger tribes, and your god will lose his people!"

Noah was silent for a moment. Then, with a shrug, he said, "God knows what he's doing. He always has a plan."

This only earned him a sigh and another shake of the head by Arishat. "I'll never get you people. Gods make mistakes, too, you know."

She didn't understand. Her gods were different. Noah didn't feel like discussing the nature of divinity again, so he merely asked what brought her here to steer the conversation to a more pleasant topic.

"I just wanted to ask if you have something to eat for little Kalbat here. She's hungry, and the people in the city, well, you know how it is," she said. The stray's ears perked up when it heard Arishat speak its name.

Noah lowered himself to give the dog an affectionate pat on the head. "You're lucky, little one. We slaughtered a sheep last night, so you can have some fresh meat today!"

He went into his house, and Arishat's attention was caught by the ark again. Could the Israelite god truly be cruel enough to send a flood to drown His own chosen people? She had heard stories from Babylonian travelers about an angry god who had become annoyed with humanity because of their great number; the loud noise of their activity had disturbed his sleep. But a different god who liked the humans stepped in and offered the solution of making men mortal, so the old ones would die when the young ones grew up and there would never be too great a number of humans in the world.

The god of the Israelites was supposed to be the friendly kind, or at least that's what Arishat thought. He was their creator. He loved them. Why would he do such a thing? It made no sense to her.

"You're still fascinated by the ship, I see," said Noah, who had returned from his house and fed Kalbat a generous cut of mutton.

"I don't believe it," she said, shaking her head. "Why would your god do this to you?"

Noah smiled. He always smiled when talking about his God and the plans He had. Arishat found Noah's attitude mildly irritating.

"Because His people are sinful and evil, Arishat," Noah said. "You know how they treat you. You should understand."

She lowered her head, eyes closed. "There are many bad people among them, yes. Sinful? I know how sinful they are. Half the city has paid for a night with me, most of them married men. But they're not evil. Not even those who insult me every day. They may not be nice people, but they have friends and families. There is a tiny little spark of goodness within each of them."

"Is that enough?" Noah asked. "Our God is perfect. Why should we, his creatures, be so imperfect? He wants to start anew and destroy a flawed creation so he can remake us without sin."

"Your people feel so superior to us Canaanites because of your almighty god," she said, her voice thick with scorn. "But I would rather have imperfect gods that make mistakes than ... this."

Noah went silent. He knew Arishat didn't like his God because she didn't understand Him, and he didn't want to upset her any further.

Finally, she sighed. "I need a drink. Gotta spend the money I make whoring on something. Right? Your god probably hates me for this."

"He doesn't—"

"I'll be in Jabez's tavern. See you later, old friend."

She turned and went away without throwing another glance at her Noah and his giant boat.

*She will never understand*, Noah thought to himself as he watched Arishat's form become smaller against the horizon.

#

Kalbat followed her as she made her way towards the tavern not far from the city walls. It was close to the gate, right beside the major trader's road— the perfect place for attracting customers.

"You're with me again, little girl? I think we should find a home for you. You'll be much happier with someone to look after you," Arishat said to the stray wagging its tail at her voice's encouraging tone. "Maybe you can stay with Jabez. He's a good man, and rich enough to feed you well."

She entered the tavern and approached the bar, where Jabez's wife Judith was cleaning last night's used mugs. There were no guests yet at this early hour.

"Hey there, Judith. Is Jabez around?"

Judith looked up from her work and greeted her guest with a smile. "He's in the back room. Do you want something from him?"

Arishat nodded and pointed to the dog sitting obediently beside her. For a stray, it was surprisingly well-behaved. "Yes. I'd like to ask if he could give a home to this dog. She deserves better than crawling from house to house begging for food."

Judith grinned. She obviously liked the idea of adopting Kalbat. "Oh, having a dog would be nice! Wait here, I'll fetch my husband."

Arishat took a seat and scratched the dog behind the ears. "You're getting a home, my little girl! Are you excited? Oh, yes, you're excited! Who's happy to finally get a master? You're happy!"

Kalbat jumped, wagged her tail, and licked Arishat's face. Of course, she didn't understand what was going on, but she noticed her favorite human's excitement and couldn't help but feel excited too.

This changed instantly when Jabez entered the room.

The dog became tense and growled, moving backwards to put more distance between the man and herself. Arishat was puzzled. Kalbat never behaved like this, not even towards people who kicked and spat at her. There seemed to be something about Jabez that she instinctively disliked.

"What's up, little girl? You don't have to worry, Jabez is a nice man."

"Yes, your friend is right, little doggie," Jabez said in a cheerful voice, which he thought would calm the dog. "I'd be happy to give you a home and provide for you. No need to fear!" Kalbat's growls grew fiercer. She barked. When the innkeeper tried to approach her, the bitch bolted, running out of the building as fast as she could.

"Well, that's strange," muttered Arishat. "She never behaves like that."

Jabez shrugged. "I've been down in the cellar all morning. It's a little musty down there, so maybe the smell put her off. Now, what can I do for you?"

"I'm in the mood for a drink. Give me wine or beer, whatever you have to offer. Just give me something with a kick."

A broad grin appeared on his face. He knew that Arishat could afford the finest of drinks and didn't mind paying the price for them. "Oh, I have just the thing for you. Yesterday, we received a shipment of excellent Minoan wine ..."

#

It had been a usual day at the tavern, with the Canaanite whore arriving early for a drink, some travelers coming in for lunch during the day, and the regulars arriving in the evening to end their day with a beer and good company. His wife was still at the tavern serving the few remaining guests who liked to stay and drink into the latest hours of the night, but Jabez was working on more important things.

He would have loved to use the stray dog the whore had brought along, but for some reason the bitch had run away. It didn't matter. He had a pig to work with, and that was just as good as a dog.

He took a bowl of water and put in a few drops of the precious fluid he experimented with, but not too many as he didn't know what effects a higher dose might have. With the pigeon, three drops had been enough to transform it into a thing of beauty, a white bird he had named *dove*. A pig would likely need more. Possibly five, or even ten.

The cooing of the transformed pigeons in their cage near the entrance announced the arrival of his wife.

"Ah, Judith. The guests have all gone home?"

"Yes, I've closed the tavern for the night." She went to the table where her husband carefully dripped little drops of red into a bowl of water. When she went to insert a finger into the mixture, Jabez grabbed her hand and pulled it away.

"Don't!" he admonished. "We have no idea what it would do to a human."

"We've seen what it can do to a pigeon. Why not just drink it ourselves?"

He shook his head. "Pigeons are birds. They have wings. I want to try it on other animals first. What if it kills you, or worse, transforms you into something hideous? We can't risk it."

Judith sighed. There was a hint of fear in her eyes. She didn't like waiting so long. "What if Noah is telling the truth? What if God really wants to send a flood to punish us for our sins?"

Jabez scoffed. "I don't believe it. And even if he does, if our experiments work, we'll have a way out. And besides, we're good people. We've always been good people. If there is anyone God would spare, it would be us."

While he took the bowl and put it in front of the pig, encouraging it to drink with a pat on the head, Judith looked at the pigeons. Or doves, as they called them. People used to call pigeons the rats of the skies. These birds were white and pure and beautiful. What if she were to drink of that precious fluid? Would her skin become smoother, her hair softer?

No, Jabez was right. It was too dangerous. They had only tested it on birds. What if it didn't work on other animals?

The pig squealed as its transformation began. Short, stubby wings sprouted from its shoulders, featherless protrusions of bone and skin. Its bristly hide couldn't decide whether to grow paler or brighter, turning a mottled pink in the process. The shrieks and grunts became more and more panicked as the pig's body mutated into a grotesque caricature of God's creation. After the transformation, its features reminded her more of a demon than of an angel.

"The poor thing," Judith gasped, visibly shaken by the display she had witnessed.

"Maybe it didn't work because pigs are unclean," Jabez mused. "We have to try it on other animals."

"What if it doesn't work at all?" Judith collapsed to the floor, sobbing. Her husband put a hand on her shoulder to comfort her.

"Don't worry," he said. "It worked with the pigeons. There's no reason it couldn't work with other creatures. The pig was just a bad choice. Don't worry, my love."

With tears in her eyes, she replied, "What if God sends the flood and our plan doesn't work? We will drown, just like all the others. We'll—"

"Shh," he whispered, gently laying a finger over her lips. "We will succeed, my dearest Judith. God's flood doesn't matter to us. We have the divine power of creation in our hands."

He hugged her and held her tight, a confident smile on his lips.

They were like gods. They had nothing to fear.

#

Arishat sat on the roof of her house, gazing into the endless sea of stars above her. The Babylonians could read the will of the gods from the movements of these celestial bodies. There were so many of them. How could the Israelites believe that the entirety of heaven and earth had been created by a single god?

A small cloud moved across the sky, partially obscuring the stars. Not long after the cloud had appeared, a light drizzle started to fall.

"It's raining," Arishat said. "Won't you come and shelter me?"

Argurios sat down beside her. "I'm your client, not your husband. If you want to cuddle, you'll have to pay," he replied with a grin.

She rolled her eyes. "Oh, come on. You're more than a client to me. You're also my friend."

"Ah, but I still have to pay for sex."

"You know that's different. I must take money for that because it's my job."

Argurios shook his head and sighed. "Why are we still doing this?"

"What do you mean?"

"Trying to carve out a life for ourselves in this gods-forsaken town. The people don't accept us. You're a whore who has to sell her body to make a living, and I barely manage to sell any of my bronze crafts because nobody here wants to buy from someone they deem an idolater."

"I guess we both have our reasons for leaving our homes behind and trying our luck elsewhere. And this town isn't that bad a place once you get used to it."

Argurios shook his head again. "Not that bad? Arishat, I know how they treat you. I've seen them just this morning throw rotten fruit at you and call you names,. How can you say this isn't a bad place?"

"Some people are decent," she answered, taking Argurios' hand in hers with a smile. "Like you, for example. But tell me, why these thoughts all of a sudden? I know you have it just as hard as I do, but you've never complained before."

He stared into the sky, silent for a while. Then he answered, "I wonder how long we have left to live. You know, with the flood and all. I wonder if life would've been better for me elsewhere. some place where the gods are friendlier."

"Are you scared of the rain, Argurios?" She laughed. "I don't believe their god would send a great flood to drown the entire country. Even if the people are sinful, they're his chosen tribe. If you were a god, would you annihilate your own worshippers for a reason like that?"

He shrugged. "The people here are unfriendly and cruel, so why shouldn't their god be the same?"

"As I said, I don't believe it. If he's truly going to send a flood, there must be a better reason than merely his people being sinful."

They sat on the roof for a little while, staring into the sky where the brightest of the stars poked through the clouds, casting a dim light unto the earth below. The rainfall was so light, Arishat could barely feel its touch upon her skin. The atmosphere was romantic.

She leaned and kissed Argurios.

"What—"

"Shh, don't say anything." She kissed him again. "Just enjoy the moment."

That night, she would not request any payment from him. He had become more than a client. He had become more than a friend.

#

The next morning, after she had said goodbye to Argurios and dressed herself, Arishat set out to Jabez's tavern again. For her, a good day always started with a drink, and considering what happened between her and Argurios last night, she considered this a day worthy of starting with the best wine she could afford.

When she went out on the streets, she found them to be almost deserted. It was still drizzling, barely enough to form a few puddles on the ground, but it seemed to keep the people inside their homes. Arishat didn't encounter anyone on her way to the tavern. Maybe they were afraid this could be the beginning of the great flood.

When she arrived at the tavern, she was surprised to find the doors locked.

That was strange. Jabez always opened his tavern early in the morning. She knocked at the door, calling his name.

"Jabez? Are you there? Judith? Anyone?" she yelled, but no one answered.

Arishat began to worry. They lived in the upper floor of the tavern, and at this time of day they should be at home, either down in the tavern or still in their bedroom. Did anything happen to them? She had to make sure they were all right. Jabez was one of the few people in town who always treated her nicely. Besides, he was her most reliable supplier of booze.

She went to the back of the tavern and checked the door there. It was unlocked. Picked open by a thief, perhaps, or maybe they forgot to lock it.

Arishat opened the door and went inside. "Hello?" she called, but apart from her own echo, nothing came back. She went upstairs to check out their bedroom, but it was empty. They were gone.

What had happened here?

"Maybe it's something down in the basement," she muttered to herself. "The way Kalbat reacted to him, he said it might've been the smell from working in the basement for so long."

She decided to check it out. What if Jabez was working on something dangerous down there and there had been an accident? She descended the stairs to the ground floor, went into the back room and climbed down into the cellar. There, she found the one thing she hadn't expected at all. One of the wine racks lining the wall had been pushed aside, revealing a secret passage.

It entered a long tunnel that led, if her sense of direction was correct, away from the city. Why would this be here? Where could it lead?

There was only one way to find out. She stepped into the tunnel and followed it as far as it went. It seemed to stretch on forever. When she reached a reinforced wooden door, it felt like she had walked for at least a quarter of an hour. She knelt in front of the door and put her ear to it.

On the other side of the room, the voices of Jabez and Judith were talking, but she couldn't make out the words. There were sounds of animals, too. The cooing of pigeons, the whinny of a horse.

Arishat had a bad feeling about this. Something strange was going on down here. She went back the way she came before they discovered she was there. This was something she had to investigate later.

For some reason, she felt that Kalbat's hostile reaction to Jabez had had something to do with whatever was happening behind that door.

#

"God will punish you for this," the angel said as Jabez drew his blood again.

"No, he won't," Jabez smiled. "I have never broken a single commandment. I have always lived by God's laws. I'm helpful even towards people who don't deserve it. There is no sin I could be punished for."

"And yet you chain me here to use me for your sick experiments. You're playing God, and you think He would not care?"

Jabez laughed. "God never gave us any rules on how to treat an angel! But you know what he said to us? You are the crown of my creation, go forth and be the masters of the earth. And that's exactly what I'm doing, nothing more and nothing less."

The angel spat on the floor. "You twist and turn the rules as you see fit. This is not God's law. This is your own sick perversion of it."

Jabez offered the angel an innocent smile. "I'm free of sin, my friend. I don't feel any guilt about what I'm doing. God created us in His own image, and I merely strive to be as close to that image as I can. God is the creator of life. I am a creator of life. He made humankind the ruler of His creation, and that is exactly what I strive to be."

"You will burn for this," the angel muttered as his captor left the tiny chamber that imprisoned him. He was weak from the loss of blood, and there was no hope he could break the heavy links of bronze chaining him to the wall. "God will burn you for this."

"What if he's right?" asked Judith as soon as her husband had left the chamber. "What if what we're doing really is wrong?"

"Don't worry, my love. We're not breaking any of God's laws," he answered, embracing her in a reassuring hug.

"I ... I don't know," she said, shaking her head. "What if the flood God is planning to send is the punishment for what we're doing? Not for everyone else being sinful, but for us."

"That's nonsense," Jabez replied with a laugh. "Don't you see? We're good people, and God has sent us the means to escape this punishment, just like he has told Noah to build his giant boat. Only we have something much better than a boat."

"You think God meant for us to capture the angel?"

He nodded. "Of course, he did. With his blood, we can create a creature that will fly us away from here as soon as the flood strikes. It's all part of God's plan, I'm sure of it."

Judith nodded, wanting to believe her husband's words. But she wasn't sure about it. They were interfering in God's creation, and that couldn't be right. Could it?

"Let's go back to the tavern and open up for business now," he said. "We'll try the blood on some other animals tonight."

#

"I'm really starting to hate this place. The rain is getting stronger, the only people who came into my shop today were here to tell me that it's all my fault for worshipping idols, and to top it all off, somebody stole my horse," Argurios complained.

"Your horse was stolen?" Arishat asked, surprised.

"Yeah. And you know what's the craziest about this? Whoever took my horse left a bag of coins in the stable. These Israelites are insane, just like their damned god."

"I didn't even know you had a horse," she said, still surprised.

"I did. It was a present from the wanax of Mycenae, back when I was in his service. It was merely a foal when I received it. Took care of it ever since." His voice was shaking. It was obvious that he was very attached to that horse.

"You never told me much about your past, Argurios," Arishat said, putting a hand on his arm as an affectionate gesture. "What did you do back in your homeland?"

He sighed and shook his head. "Something I ran away from for a reason. I'm sorry, I don't want to talk about my past. Not yet, at least."

"It's okay. I understand," she replied, followed by a kiss. "I don't like to talk about my past either."

He grunted, which was his version of a nod.

"And I don't have the time to talk right now, anyway. There's something I must do," she added. "We'll meet again later."

Argurios grinned. "What, are you meeting a client? You can tell me, Arishat. It's what you do for a living; there's no need to be that vague about it."

"No, my dear. I'm not meeting a client," she said, shaking her head. "There's something else. Something I must check out."

#

The drizzle had now turned into a proper, real rainfall. By the time she had reached the tavern, her dress was wet, and her hair was dripping with water. Luckily, the tavern was open now. She wouldn't have wanted to have made that journey in vain.

"Arishat! What are you doing outside in this weather?" Jabez asked as she entered. "You'll get sick letting yourself get this wet!"

Arishat greeted the innkeeper with a smile. "Hey, you know I need my drink in the morning. I came by earlier, when the rain was merely a drizzle, but your doors were closed."

Jabez put a clay mug on the bar counter and reached for an amphora. "We had a long day yesterday, so my wife and I decided to open up a little later than usual." He poured some wine from the amphora into the mug. "Here, have a drink on the house to make it up to you."

"Thanks. Every time I come here, you remind me why I keep coming back," she said. She took a seat at the bar and gratefully accepted the free mug of wine.

She enjoyed her drink and talked about the latest rumors with Jabez, just as she always did when she came here. But now she knew that something was going on, something that Jabez kept secret. In truth, this was the real reason she had come here, to see what Jabez would say when she mentioned the tavern having been closed earlier. He hadn't told her the entire truth, and she had the strange feeling that he was hiding something terrible.

"Well, that's it for today," she said after she had finished her drink. "See you tomorrow."

"Leaving already? It's still raining outside."

"Yes, but I don't think it'll stop anytime soon. And I have some things to do, so I better get home now. Busy day. Well, you know how it is," she said with a wink.

He smiled at her as she left, a friendly smile that was so typical of him. But deep in his eyes she could see something entirely different. She saw contempt.

She realized that it had always been there.

#

Arishat had to find out what Jabez was hiding, so she followed the underground tunnel. There hadn't been any twists or turns, as she remembered it, but she hoped to find something if she walked long enough.

With every step, water spilled into her sandals and mud oozed between her toes. The heavy rain made it hard to see, yet she walked on. After what felt like an eternity, she finally found an abandoned tower in the fields, far enough from the city and the roads to attract no attention. When she approached the door of the tower, she wasn't surprised to find it locked and bolted from the inside. It was fashioned from thick, heavy wood and she couldn't imagine even the strongest of men breaking it open. She had to find another way inside. She circled the tower a couple of times, trying to think of a good way to infiltrate it, before noticing windows in the upper floors. The walls were rough and irregular, with holes and protruding stones that could serve as footholds.

"This has to be the dumbest idea you've ever had," she said aloud, slipping her hand into a hole in the stonework. She pulled herself up, bracing a foot against the wall. She slipped, falling into the mud. With a groan, she pulled herself up from the ground and untied her sandals. When she had bared her feet, she attempted the climb again. "Curiosity and stubbornness, one day they will get me killed."

This time, she managed to keep her balance. She almost fell again when a stone broke loose under her foot. The rain beat against her back and with each step her arms grew heavier.

"Dear gods, don't forsake me now."

When she reached the window, she pulled herself through and fell to the floor on the other side. When she gathered enough strength, she stood and descended the stairs into the basement. It was larger than she expected it to be.

"Could you be the horse that was stolen from Argurios?" There were other animals too, mostly birds. The strangest were kept in a large cage together. They looked like pigeons, but their feathers were pure white, almost divine.

An opening led to another room. She stepped through and encountered a tall man with pale skin and black hair chained to the wall. On his back were wings larger than any bird she had ever seen.

"What ... who ... what are you?"

The man looked up, a defeated expression on his face. His eyes glowed as if a lit candle were behind them. They had lost all glimmer of hope. "My name is Lucifer. I'm an angel of God."

"An angel? How did you get here? What happened to you?"

"I was sent by God to bring elucidation to His people, for he thought they deserved it. I was to be the lightbringer, the one to carry divine knowledge and the message of God's love to His people. That was many months ago."

"You've been chained here for months?" Arishat couldn't imagine that Jabez would do that to such a magnificent creature.

"Yes. The first human I met here on earth was a man named Jabez. At first, he acted friendly towards me and showed much hospitality. He invited me to his home, but now I'm not even sure whether this is his home at all. I'm not sure what happened next. My memory is a blur. He brought me here and somehow managed to knock me out. When I woke up, I found myself in chains."

"Why would he do this to you? I can't believe Jabez is keeping you here like this. He has always been—" she began, then she remembered that look in his eyes. Beneath Jabez's friendly demeanor was something bad, maybe evil. "I always thought he was a good person."

Lucifer nodded. "Yes. And he really believes he is. He doesn't see anything wrong with what he's doing."

"But why? What does he want from you?"

"My blood," the angel grimaced.

Arishat's eyes widened. "Your blood?"

"Yes. The blood of an angel contains the divine essence of God's creation. Jabez uses this divine essence to shape new creatures and thinks himself a god because of it."

"Oh, no. No, no, no." Arishat's whole body began to shake. This changed everything. This meant that God actually had a reason to punish his people. An angel sent from heaven to bring enlightenment and love, treated like this by the first human he met.

"Did you see those white birds in the other room? He fed my blood to a couple of pigeons. This is what became of them," Lucifer said.

God didn't have to punish His entire people for the actions of one man. This was wrong. All of it was wrong. Arishat decided she had to do something about it. She had to make this right.

"I'm going to set you free," she said. "I don't know how, but I'll find a way. I promise."

"Thank you, young woman," the angel replied with a smile. After months of captivity, he finally saw a glimmer of hope again. "After meeting Jabez, I thought that God was wrong about you. You humans don't deserve His love. Thank you for showing me that there are still some who do."

Arishat had to chuckle, despite the seriousness of the situation. "He's not my god," she said.

"What do you mean?" Lucifer asked, confused.

"It doesn't matter. Listen, I'll find a way to break your chains. Then I'm going to come back. But for now, I should get out of here before your captors return. If Jabez finds me here, I'll end up in chains just like you," she said. "Hold on to your hope. I'll be back."

She left the angel and ran up the stairs to the tower's ground floor where she quickly unbolted the door and stepped outside. She let herself collapse to the soft, muddy ground. After what she had seen, she welcomed the cool drops of rain on her skin, the water from the heavens washing away the filth of the basement.

Jabez kept a creature of God in captivity to harvest its blood. Behind his friendly face, there was a sick mind without any sense of morality. For this, God would send a flood to drown his people.

Arishat cried. Her tears mingled with those wept by the heavens.

#

When she stepped through the city gates, Arishat was a mess. Her long hair hung in wet strands over her face, her dress was soaked, and her bare feet were covered in mud. She shouldn't have been so stupid, so thoughtless. She could've taken the horse to ride to the city, but she hadn't thought of that when she started her journey. She could've put her sandals on, but she had forgotten about those, too. Now, she was dirty and exhausted and still not one step further in finding a solution. She had no idea how to free the angel from his shackles.

At least the water on the streets washed away the mud on her feet. What had started as a drizzle last night was now a torrent, and the rain had been going for hours now. Some people, knowing it wouldn't stop, walled up their doors and windows to keep the water out of their homes. Only a few still doubted God's wrath.

Had she not seen what was going on in the abandoned tower, Arishat would have been among these few.

Finally, she reached her house. As soon as she opened the door, the water from the street spilled inside. Closing it didn't help in keeping it out, either. Some water came through the door crack.

"That's just great." she muttered. Not having any better idea, she went to her wardrobe to search for a blanket or any sufficiently large piece of cloth to put in front of the door. That would at least soak up some of the water spilling in.

After all that mud and rain, the one thing she wanted most right now was a hot bath followed by a long sleep in a dry bed.

That plan was interrupted by a knock at the door.

"Yes? Who's there?"

"Arishat," said a familiar voice, "I thought I'd stop by and help you out."

That voice made a smile appear on her lips, and she was more than happy to open the door. "Argurios! Your company is just what I need right now.

Come in!"

He was shocked to see her disheveled. "By Zeus, where have you been? You look like you've walked through a swamp."

"I just came back from the tavern and was surprised by the rain," she said with a dismissive wave of her hand. "It is a lot heavier compared to this morning."

The look Argurious gave her indicated that he didn't believe a few minutes in the rain could make her look like this.

"So, what do you want to help me with?" Arishat hoped the question would divert his attention away from her condition. She didn't want to involve him with the captured angel. She'd rather keep Argurios out of danger.

"I thought I could put some bricks in your windows and doorway to keep out the water. Most people are doing that now because it's quite obvious the great flood is coming. This way, we'll at least stay dry for a few more days," he answered.

"And how would I leave my house if the doorway is walled off?" she asked, implying she found the idea to be rather silly.

"Well, I use a ladder from the roof," Argurios said with a grin.

Arishat stared at him for a moment. That was a simple but surprisingly elegant solution, she thought. "Very well, then. Do it. I'll heat up some water so I can have a nice, long bath while you're making my house flood-proof."

"I'll get to work immediately, my dear."

"I hope so! Cause when you're done, you can give me a nice little foot massage," she teased. "I could really use one right now."

"Of course. Everything for my dear little lady."

#

When Argurios climbed down from the roof to return to his home the next morning, the water on the street was at waist level. With every hour, the rainfall seemed to become heavier, a ceaseless downpour with no end in sight. Arishat still had no idea how she could free the angel.

The chains were made of solid bronze. They were set into the wall, which

109

was made of solid stone. And now that the flood was rising ever higher, Jabez would likely spend more time in the tower than in his tavern. If he caught her sneaking in, he could easily overpower her.

She could have asked Argurios for help, but she didn't want to endanger the man she loved. No, this was something she had to do alone. But no matter how much she thought about it, she couldn't think of a way to save Lucifer.

"Damn you, Arishat," she muttered to herself. "Damn you and your desire to always do the right thing. It has ruined you once already."

With a sigh, she got out of bed and walked to where she kept the only thing left from her previous life. She couldn't find an answer on her own, so it was time to turn to her gods. It was a long time ago that she had served as their priestess, but she worshipped them with as much piety now as she did all those years ago.

If she couldn't find an answer on her own, the gods would take her hand and lead her on the right path. They had never failed her before.

#

Jabez was no longer an innkeeper. His inn was gone. He had walled off the entrance to the basement to keep the water from flooding the tunnel, but he hadn't bothered to protect the tavern itself. His old life was over, and his new life would soon begin. He would be far away from here, creating his own Eden. His creations would rival those of God himself.

His heart swelled with pride as he beheld the creatures he had made. The effects of the angelic blood were as varied as God's creation itself. The lizards he had fed with it had grown featherless wings and gained the ability to breathe fire. The pigeons had turned into white birds of purest beauty. A squirrel he had caught in the woods had grown large furry membranes between its limbs that allowed it to glide in the air.

"What if it doesn't work on the horse?" his wife asked, her voice trembling with fear. She was afraid they would end up stuck here and drown like all the others.

"Don't worry, my dear. Of course, it'll work. This angel is God's gift to us so we can escape the punishment of the wicked. I'm sure God knew we'd find a horse to use the blood on. Just imagine, a winged horse, an even better means of escape than Noah's silly boat, don't you think?" he replied, dismissing her worries.

"We didn't find the horse," she said. "We stole it."

Jabez slapped his wife across the cheek. "We didn't steal anything!" he yelled.

"Jabez, stop! You're hurting me!"

"I'm sorry," he said. His wife was the only person he truly cared about, and he didn't want to lash out against her. "We didn't steal the horse, Judith. We paid for it. We never broke God's law. It wasn't theft."

"I'm scared, Jabez. I'm scared of the flood. I'm scared that God doesn't approve of what we're doing. I'm just scared," she said, tears streaming down her cheeks.

The last few months had been hard on her, and with the advent of the flood it had only become worse. She had so many doubts about working with the angelblood, but Jabez knew how he could show her that what they did was right, that it was all part of God's plan. God knew they were better than all these liars and adulterers and hypocrites in the city, and sending the angel was His reward for their virtue. He wanted them to become like gods themselves, because they were the only humans worthy of becoming the true image of the creator.

"Judith, my dearest Judith, you don't have to be afraid," he said, soothing her with a gentle touch on the cheek, wiping away her tears. "We'll try the blood on the horse, and then you'll see. It will work, and then you'll see that God is on our side."

She nodded. He smiled.

He took a bottle of the precious fluid and poured it into the horse's trough. For an animal of that size, this seemed to be the correct dosage. He tried to encourage it to drink, but the horse grew nervous when he got too close. Jabez took a few steps back and waited.

After a while, the horse drank.

As the transformation started to happen, the horse kicked about wildly. Its brown coat turned ivory white, and large feathered wings sprouted from its back, as beautiful as the angel's own. The change was complete in a few minutes.

"It worked!" Jabez yelled. "I told you it would work! God has given us our way out!"

"He, He did," said Judith. She almost couldn't believe it. "I'm so sorry I ever doubted you, my love. We did it."

Jabez laughed. It was a laugh born out of triumph and the knowledge of what he had become. Of what they had become. "Yes, Judith, yes. *We* did it. We don't even need God's help anymore. We have become as gods ourselves."

Her first instinct was to scold him for blaspheming God's greatness, but she knew he was right. With the blood of the angel, they held the power of creation in their hands. They had become as gods.

#

Arishat didn't know how much time she had spent in prayer and meditation, but it had to have been more than a day. When she opened the hatch in the ceiling and climbed onto her roof, she saw that the flood had risen dramatically. It was high enough to dangle her feet in the water if she sat at the edge of her roof.

There wasn't much time left. If she wanted to do the right thing, she had to act now. Another day and the flood would drown everyone. And Jabez would fly away with the help of some strange, mutated creature, escaping the punishment that was meant for him.

She went into her house again, closing the hatch to keep out the rain. She knelt in front of the statuettes placed upon her altar, calling out to her gods for help. She didn't know how she could free the angel. She didn't know how she could stop Jabez, but she knew the gods would give her what she required.

And that, in turn, required a sacrifice on her part.

"Give, and thou shalt be given," she whispered to herself as she prepared to give away the most valuable things she possessed in order to right a wrong that didn't concern her. She didn't have to do it; she could simply ask her gods to grant her a means of escape. But it wasn't in her nature to accept injustice without acting against it.

Many years ago, speaking out against a corrupt priesthood had earned her banishment and exile. She had been bribed to keep her mouth shut, but she spoke up. She had spoken up and was silenced by those more powerful than herself, and she lost her position as priestess. It had been the right thing to do. *This* was the right thing to do.

"One day, this is going to get me killed. Maybe today is that day. But it doesn't matter. Oh, greatest gods, help me in my task. Help me do what I must do," she implored as she lighted the fires of sacrifice, three large bowls of burning oil which would consume her offerings and carry them into the heavens.

This was the hardest sacrifice she had ever made. She didn't have much to give, but she was ready to give everything that mattered to her. She took the pair of scissors she had laid upon the altar, pulled up a strand of her hair and cut it close to the scalp. Then another, and another. Lock by lock, her long tresses fell to the ground. Tears streamed down her cheeks as she chopped off what she adored most about herself.

She didn't have much to give, but she was willing to give it all.

When nothing but a short, uneven stubble remained, she gathered up her fallen locks and placed them gently into a burning bowl.

"Baal-Hadad, Lord of the skies, Lord of the rain and the storms, who makes fertile the ground and strikes with lightning against your foes, accept my sacrifice and grant me the help I need. Baal-Hadad, Lord of the skies, show me a way to put an end to Jabez's evil and make right the wrongs he has done."

To the flames of the second bowl, she fed her dresses, the beautiful cloth that made her desirable to the men of the city. For years, making herself appealing to men had been the way of her life. Now, she gave it all away.

"Shapash, Lady of the Sun, torch of the gods, oh great goddess who gives light and warmth unto the earth, accept my sacrifice, and grant me the help I need. Great Shapash, Lady of the Sun, give me the tools I need to put an end to Jabez and his vile deeds."

Finally, she took off her jewelry and threw it into the third bowl. The fire shouldn't have been hot enough to melt it, but as soon as it hit the flames, it all disappeared in a puff of smoke. Not the black smoke of something burnt, but the pure, white smoke of sacrifice.

The gods had accepted her offer.

"Ashtart, oh Lady of Love, my dearest goddess, my greatest friend," she whispered, "help me in my task as you have always helped me before. You have been a light to me, an inspiration in the darkest times of my life. I have always served you faithfully, both as a qadishtu in the temple and here as a simple, mundane prostitute. Dearest Ashtart, lend me your guidance so that

I may succeed."

For a long time, Arishat knelt motionless in front of the altar, the fires of sacrifice illuminating her tear-stained face. There were no ashes in the bowls; her offerings had gone up into the heavens where they had been received by the gods.

The fires went out, extinguished by a swift gust of wind, the breath of Baal-Hadad leaving her in the darkness of her walled-up house. The only source of light left was a small candle she had placed upon the altar. It had been spared by Hadad's breath.

Arishat stood and went around to behind the altar where she found the answer to her prayers. From her sacrifice, the gods had fashioned a bow for her; the bow itself was made from horn the same color as her hair, strong and flexible. The string was made from finest cloth, woven so tightly as to be unbreakable. The arrows were made of gold, with tips of many-colored precious stones.

Now she knew what she had to do. She had to slay Jabez before he could escape his judgement. She had to deliver the punishment that God couldn't.

Before she went on her way, she placed the statuettes of her gods into the small chest she kept them in. She couldn't leave them here where they would sink in the flood. She had to give them into the hands of someone she could trust.

They were the only things she had left of her old life. Besides, they were sacred to her, and she couldn't just leave her own gods to drown.

After she had replaced the statuettes and closed the chest, she broke her furniture and tore apart the only piece of clothing she had left to fashion a makeshift raft. It wasn't much, but it was enough to reach the tower where Jabez was hiding.

First, she would pay a short visit to a friend.

#

"Arishat?" Argurios murmured to himself as he spotted the raft approaching his home. It couldn't be. The woman on the raft looked so different. A beggar, possibly, clad in nothing but a ragged loincloth. As she drew closer, he realized it was her, after all. "Arishat! By all the gods, what happened to you?"

She maneuvered the raft close to his house and placed a small chest on his roof.

"Argurios, I came to give you this and to say goodbye if we never meet again. I don't know whether I'm going to return from where I'm going."

He was so shocked by her appearance that he didn't realize what she had said. "What happened to your hair? Why are you naked? Arishat, who did this to you?"

"Argurios, my love, listen." She didn't intend to answer any of his questions. She couldn't involve him in this. She didn't want him to get hurt. "There is something I must do. I can't tell you what, but it's important. You must believe me."

"What do you mean? Where are you going?"

She pointed to the chest. "In this chest, there is something from my past that is important to me. I couldn't leave it in my house to get lost in the flood. Please, look out for it. Maybe this rain will cease, and we will all survive and I will come back. But please, just keep it close and think of me."

"Arishat, damn you, tell me what's going on!" he yelled.

Arishat looked saddened. "No, I can't. I don't want to get you involved. I, I don't want you to endanger yourself. I know it's ridiculous, but I don't want you to get hurt because of me. I must do this alone."

"Endanger myself? Arishat, do you know who I am? If there is anything that is dangerous to me, it would be even more dangerous to you! Wherever you're going, I'm coming with you," he said.

She smiled. It was a smile of sadness. But there was something else in it, too. There was love, and a deep gratitude for the short time the gods had allowed them together. "I love you," she said softly, turning her raft and paddling away.

"Stop! Damn you, Arishat. Stop!" Her tiny raft floated on, steady on its course toward the city gate.

"Damn you," he whispered. "Wherever you're going, I will come after you. And I swear by my gods, if anyone dares to hurt you—" He didn't finish the thought. He wasn't keen on getting into a fight, but if he had to do it for his beloved, he wouldn't hesitate. His beloved, of whom he knew so little and who didn't know much more about him. Would she have let him join if he had told her of his past? He looked at the chest she had left him. It contained something from her former life, she had said. He opened it and peeked inside.

"Statuettes?" He puzzled over the sight of them. "Arishat, I have no idea what you used to be before you came here. But if I want to help you in whatever you're doing, I think I must revisit my past, too."

He closed the lid and carried the chest into his house. He placed it on the ground and opened an old chest of his own. He had no desire to pick up what he had left behind so long ago. But if he had to do it for his beloved, he wouldn't hesitate.

#

Driven forward by grim determination, Arishat maneuvered her raft through the murky water until she spotted the shape of the abandoned tower in the fog. Bow and arrows in her hand, she approached the building as swiftly as her makeshift raft would allow. The water was so high that the tower appeared to be no taller than the small one-story houses of the city, jutting only a few feet out of the surface.

On top of the tower, she could see Jabez standing next to a horse with wings. She ran a hand over her shorn head and took a deep breath.

Jabez mounted the horse and reached down to his wife to help her up. Arishat stood, trying to get sure footing on her raft, and lifted her bow. Now was the moment to act. If she hesitated, Jabez would be gone.

"Jabez!" she yelled. "Jabez, you coward! I bring your righteous punishment!"

The innkeeper looked in surprise. But surprise turned to shock when he saw Arishat's raft. By then it was too late.

The arrow had been launched.

It hit Jabez in the thigh. It penetrated his flesh and entered the horse's flank without causing harm. The horse panicked and bucked its rider off, causing Jabez to fall onto the tower's roof. It snorted, whinnied, and flew away without a rider.

"No! No! You bitch, you whore, you filthy slut! Not my horse! Not my horse!"

Jabez, filled with rage, watched his means for escape disappear into the fog.

"Jabez, get down!" yelled his wife, pulling him to her as a second arrow whizzed over their heads.

Arishat smiled. The gods had given her the perfect weapon to deliver justice. The arrow had wounded Jabez, but it didn't harm the horse. These arrows would only harm the sinner himself.

Jabez and Judith descended into the tower's interior as Arishat moved the raft closer. The windows had all been bricked up, so she had to climb to the tower's roof.

"I swore I'd never do this again. Gods, give me strength!"

She used her loincloth to tie the bow and arrows tightly to her body and climbed the slick wall of the tower. This time, it was easier than before, even though the wall was more brittle due to the rainfall. When she pulled herself over the battlements and onto the roof, she forgot all about the difficulty of the climb.

She took her bow into her hand again and descended the stairs. Slowly, carefully, she checked out every room before descending another level. If Jabez managed to ambush her, she was dead. She wouldn't stand a chance against him in a fight.

When she entered the basement, she expected Jabez to be waiting for her with a club, ready to strike at her. What she didn't expect were hordes of tiny fire-spitting lizards assaulting her from all directions. They bit and clawed at her, burning her with their breath, dozens of them attacking her as if she was their next meal. In her attempt to fight them off, she dropped her bow.

Jabez took the opportunity to jump at her with a rope, tying it around her wrists, her arms, her thighs, her legs. Now, she was as helpless as the captured angel. He kicked the lizards away from her and dragged her into the room where Lucifer was chained.

The angel's eyes widened when he saw her. "You?"

Jabez grumbled. "You know her? You've seen her before?"

He threw Arishat against the wall, and when he reached for her hair to yank her up again, he noticed for the first time that it was gone. He left her lying on the ground, kicking her in the ribs and the chest and the thighs. "You filthy, sneaky little whore! You deceiving bitch! You've been here, haven't you? What did you do? Did you try to steal from me? Did you come to take what is rightfully mine?"

"Jabez, no! Please, don't be so cruel," Judith placed a hand on his shoulder.

At first, it seemed like he would turn and hit her, fueled by his anger, but then he composed himself and grinned. It was a wicked grin, the true mirror of his soul, all façade of friendliness gone.

"Yes. Yes, I have a much better idea. Bring me a bottle, my dear, and my knife."

When Judith realized what he wanted to do, she hesitated, but then she complied. She knew it would not be wise to enrage him further.

He took the knife, cut a small wound into Lucifer's arm, and filled the bottle with blood. He turned to Arishat and laughed. "What a fool I am. When you scared my horse away, I thought you had come to ruin everything I worked for. But, no, you are another gift sent to me by God!"

"The only thing your God has sent for you is the flood. It's the punishment for what you have done. Don't you see?" Arishat tried to appeal to Jabez's last shred of sanity, but it was no use.

"No, no, you don't see! Some of the experiments have failed, you know. I tried to give the angel's blood to a pig, but it turned into a grotesque monster and died from its mutations. It doesn't work the same way on every animal— the changes are always different. I didn't drink it myself because I wasn't sure what effect it would have on a human. But now I have you to test it on!"

"No! Don't you dare!"

Arishat moved her face away from the bottle Jabez tried to force upon her. He grabbed for her hair only to realize again that it was gone.

"What happened to your precious hair, you little slut? Did someone pay you to cut it off? No matter, there are other ways to keep you still." He grabbed her by the jaw. Applying pressure to her cheeks, Jabez forced Arishat's lips open and poured the angelblood into her mouth.

Once the bottle was empty, he stepped back to behold her transformation. Arishat screamed as the divine essence in the blood took its effect, changing her body to something other than human. Her skin became lighter. All bruises and blemishes vanished. Her hair thickened and softened, growing rapidly until it reached her knees. Her eyes glowed with divine light.

And from her back grew a pair of wings with feathers as white and pure as Lucifer's.

"It works! It works!" shouted Jabez, laughing madly. "Bring me a bottle, Judith! I will become like an angel, a divine being, powerful, so powerful … I …"

He didn't have the patience to wait for a bottle. He jumped at Lucifer and drank his blood directly from the wound. Lucifer, weakened from his months of captivity, sat passively as the man sucked the blood straight from the vein. Arishat, bound by the rope and shocked from her own transformation, found herself unable to act.

After he had slaked his thirst for divine essence, Jabez waited.

"No—" Arishat stretched an arm towards him. By doing so, she tore the ropes that bound her. The angelblood had infused her with a strength far beyond what she had been capable of as a human. "No! I could've stopped him. I should've stopped him."

"Don't worry," said Lucifer. "He won't get what he wished for."

When Jabez screamed, it wasn't a scream of agony like Arishat's had been. It was a scream filled with terror at the realization of what he was turning into. His skin became a dull shade of red, his beard turned into writhing snakes growing from his face, and his forehead sprouted horns like those of a goat. The wings that grew from his back were more like a bat's than an angel's.

"Jabez! No!" Judith raced to her husband, whose body trembled violently as the angelblood turned him into an ugly abomination.

"What's happening to him?" Arishat asked, confused by the reaction to the angelblood that was so very different from her own.

"His heart is evil," Lucifer replied. "And a creature of evil cannot turn into a creature of light when it is touched by divine essence. Now, fulfill your promise and set me free!"

She nodded and went for the angel. She pulled at his chains, but even with her new strength she couldn't manage to break the solid bronze.

"He has the key to my handcuffs in the pouch at his belt. Take it!" Lucifer ordered.

Arishat tore the pouch from Jabez's belt and unlocked Lucifer's cuffs. Then, she left the writhing man and his crying wife behind, climbing the tower with the angel close behind. When she had reached the top of the tower, she soared into the air, enthralled by a new, unfamiliar feeling.

At her apex, she raised her face to the sky and yelled. "Enough with this rain! Baal-Hadad, Lord of the skies, Lord of the rain and the storms, I call thy name! Clear the sky and cast away these clouds!"

The clouds scattered, allowing the sun to break through and shine her light upon the flooded earth. After hours and days of rain and fog, she could see the horizon again. But the rain did not cease entirely. The Israelite God continued to conjure storms in his wrath as Hadad fought to chase the clouds away.

Not far from the city, Arishat spotted Noah's ark drifting on the waves. There he was, enjoying the safe shelter of his boat while the people in the city sat on their rooftops waiting for the water to rise to their throats.

"Come, Lucifer! We must save them!" she said, flying towards the city.

"Save them? Didn't God send the flood to punish them for their wickedness? Why should we save those whom God wishes to destroy?"

Arishat couldn't believe how fast she could fly. She managed to cover a distance that took many minutes on foot in mere seconds through the air. It didn't take long to soar over the city.

"Because they're worth saving. Look at them, Lucifer. Do they seem wicked to you?"

From up there, she could see them all. Hafet, the man who used to spend more time with her than with his wife, sat on the rooftop of his house with his family, telling a story to his children. Benjamin, who loved to kick the poor stray, allowed Kalbat to stay on his rooftop and shared his food with her. Neighbors were chatting with each other, sharing clean water and dry blankets.

"Deep down, they are all good people. And your God, what is he for ignoring their prayers? They don't deserve to die for a crime they didn't commit. Come on, help me carry them to Noah's ark! A ship of that size can hold more than just one family." Arishat dove to the nearest rooftop.

"Very well. You showed me that there can be goodness within the hearts of humans. I'll help you." Lucifer followed her.

Together, they picked up a family and carried them to Noah's ark. The mother and father fell to their knees and kissed Arishat's feet. She didn't stay for long, however, as there were more people to save.

Noah crawled out of his cabin to check out what all that noise was about.

"What's happening here? How did all these people get here? This is my ship! God didn't intend … Arishat? By God, you're an angel!" he blurted as he watched her carry another person to the ark.

"It's a long story," Arishat replied. "You make sure these people get food and shelter. We'll talk later."

"Did God send you?" Noah asked, bowing before her angelic form. "Were you always an angel? Did He send you to test if we were good people?"

"No. He didn't send me. He still wants to drown all these people, but I don't want that. That's why I'm saving them."

Before he could question her further, she was in the air again.

"We're too slow!" she shouted to Lucifer as they circled the skies above the city. "There are so many people left, we can't save them all before the flood rises above the rooftops."

Thanks to the intervention of Baal-Hadad, the rain lightened, but the water level continued to rise and there were thousands of people to be saved. An impossible task for the two of them alone.

"Then some of them will fall to God's wrath just as he intended." Lucifer shrugged. He didn't care too much about the fate of these humans.

"But they don't deserve to die!" Arishat yelled. "They're not wicked!"

"You don't know that. Jabez appeared friendly when I first met him, and then he turned out to be an evil man. Some of them deserve their punishment."

She had to admit that the angel was right. Many of those who had always treated her badly proved they were good people now that the situation was grave and their neighbors required their help. Others just sat on rooftops, keeping large amounts of food to themselves, and not sharing with anyone. Were they bad at heart, or were they scared for their lives? Who could judge who was good and who was evil?

"Lucifer, I have an idea," Arishat said after giving it some thought. "I'll fly back to the tower and fetch all these bottles that Jabez filled with your blood. We could pour them into the water, so everyone who swallows it will either grow the wings of an angel or die painfully, depending on whether they're good or evil."

"What? No, wait! This is madness! You cannot tamper with God's creation in this way!" Lucifer yelled, but she was already on the way to the tower. He followed her.

When Arishat approached the tower, she was met with something she hadn't expected. Jabez had survived his transformation and stood on the tower's roof, flapping his leathery wings. He took off into the air towards her.

"You Canaanite whore!" The snakes on his chin writhed and squirmed. "You cursed me, you and your devilish gods! You stole the blessing that was to be mine!"

"I stole nothing," Arishat said. "It is the evil within your heart that made you what you are."

"Liar! You worship false gods and sell your body to the highest bidder. There is no creature more wicked than you! I know what you did to me. You placed a curse upon me. You cut your hair before you came to my tower. A Babylonian merchant once told me that witches use human hair for their spells. You used your evil Canaanite magic on me to steal what was rightfully mine." His eyes glowed red with rage.

Jabez, furious, launched himself at Arishat, screaming and spitting and roaring like a demon who had escaped from the deepest pits of the underworld. Arishat was too slow to evade, and he hit her square in the chest, pushing her back a couple of feet. She tumbled and barely managed to regain her balance before hitting the water.

Jabez was full of hate and anger. Arishat didn't think she stood a chance against him.

"Jabez!" Lucifer screamed, descending upon the innkeeper. "You captured me! You tortured me for months! You will pay for this, you monster!"

Jabez laughed as he allowed Lucifer to collide with him. He closed his arms around the angel, spun in the air to gather momentum and threw Lucifer onto the tower where he landed with an audible *crack*.

"Foolish angel, what do you think you are? I have become a god, and you were merely my tool!" Jabez laughed. The snakes on his chin danced. "And now for you, whore. I will make you suffer for the curse you cast upon me. I will pluck every feather from your wings and every hair from your head, you little witch."

Arishat and Jabez circled each other, each observing the other's movements. Then, Jabez leaped at her, striking her chest with a taloned hand. The attack tore deep into the soft flesh of her breasts. She hit him back but didn't so much as bruise him.

And so it went, a strike by a taloned hand followed by a punch, a punch followed by a kick, an awkward dodge, another strike, another scratch, a bleeding wound. Arishat knew she couldn't win. Jabez was relentless, and the claws on his monstrous hands effortlessly sliced through her naked flesh. After all she went through, she would fail in stopping the man responsible for the flood.

Suddenly, Arishat felt a gust of wind and heard the sound of bronze slashing against flesh followed by a scream. It was Jabez's voice she heard above the fray.

"Arishat," a familiar voice shouted, "when this is over, you'll better explain to me what happened to you and to my horse!"

Argurios was the last person she would have expected to see, but there he was, astride his winged horse, clad in a shining armor of bronze, gold, and silver. In his right hand he held a sword, the weapon of a noble warrior. It was the most beautiful sight she could imagine.

"Argurios! Behind you!" A swarm of small, winged lizards ascended from the tower, flying straight towards Argurios and his horse. Judith must have unleashed them to help her husband.

And then, everything seemed to happen at once. Argurios turned to face the tiny fire-breathers, Lucifer took off into the air again, though he was too weak to be of any help in the fight, and Jabez seized the moment to launch himself towards Argurios.

This went too far. Arishat bore the wounds of combat without complaint, but she couldn't allow Jabez to hurt the man she loved. She was no fighter, and she couldn't stop him, but she used to be a priestess and her gods could help.

"Shapash, Lady of the Sun, torch of the gods, I call thy name! Strike down this demon with your fire, send your rays of light to set him ablaze with purifying flames!"

Arishat's prayer was answered.

A single ray of light shot from the sun, a lance of scorching heat so strong it seared Arishat's foe. Jabez lit up like an oil lamp, screaming as he burned. The dragons that attacked Argurios' steed retreated into the tower, terrified of the screaming monstrosity that tumbled through the air.

At that moment, Lucifer threw himself at Jabez. In his rage against his former captor, he hadn't seen the ray of light, and he only noticed that his foe was aflame when he himself had caught on fire. Together, they fell from the sky as a burning bundle of rage, still fighting each other, each knowing they were near the end. They plunged into the floodwater and the fire went out.

"Lucifer, no!"

Arishat lowered her head and shed a tear for the innocent angel who had suffered so much. He would have deserved a better end than this.

After a few moments, he surfaced again. His hair was gone, his skin covered in burn marks, and his wings had become featherless lumps of flesh, but he wasn't dead.

"Lucifer, you survived!"

"My wings! I've lost my wings!" Lucifer screamed. "It's all your fault, betrayer!"

"What?" By now, Arishat didn't think anything could surprise her anymore. But Lucifer claiming she betrayed him? That was ridiculous.

"You called upon your goddess to burn Jabez just as I threw myself at him! You are no better than him, none of you are better. God was right to punish your kind for your wickedness. You are betrayers, deceivers, sinners, all of you!"

"I didn't know you were about to attack him! It wasn't on purpose," Arishat defended herself.

"No more of your human lies. There is no goodness within you. You all

124

deserve the worst fate you can get. You!" Lucifer yelled, pointing at Judith, who had ascended the tower and stared into the water at the spot where her beloved Jabez had gone down. "Why don't you join your dear husband? What is your life without him? You have no reason to go on, woman. Everyone will know you were responsible for the flood. You will live as an outcast. Go, join your husband in death! It is the best fate you can hope for."

"Lucifer, what are you doing?" Arishat asked. "Don't make her—"

It was too late. Judith had stabbed herself with the same dagger Jabez had used to cut Lucifer. She let her lifeless body fall into the water so her corpse could rest next to her husband's.

"You humans have tortured and betrayed me. This is how I will deal with all of you from now on. Even if you survive and find dry land to settle, I shall return and plague your kind for all eternity. It is all you deserve for what you have done to me." And he vanished beneath the waves and dived away.

The heavens weeped, drowning the earth in tears of rage.

"Enough of this. Enough death, enough suffering," cried Arishat. "Yahweh, God of the Israelites, I call thy name! What kind of god are you to punish an entire tribe for the crimes of one man? Show compassion and cease this senseless rain! Your people deserve a better fate than this. Do you not see that your judgement is wrong? In the face of death, all these people, no matter how cruel they had been before, are now showing their good side by helping their neighbors, even though they know it is pointless. At the same time, a creature of divinity, one of your own angels, turns to evil because of the things that happened to him. There is goodness in the hearts of men, and evil in the hearts of the divine. Show mercy to your people! Many of them are better than the angel you just lost."

There was nothing but silence.

Then, the clouds cleared, and large, glowing letters appeared in the sky in the language of the Israelites.

*I am the Lord, your God. You shall fear no evil for I am your shepherd. I will guide you to a new home where you shall live in peace, and no harm shall ever befall you. I shall love you as my own sons, and I will be like a heavenly father unto you. Amen.*

"So, this means he forgives them?" asked Argurios, seated on his flying horse.

"I think so," Arishat answered. "He's a strange god, but I guess he understood the point I was making."

Suddenly, the tower where Jabez had conducted his angelblood experiments collapsed, and from the rubble emerged the white pigeons he had created.

Arishat nodded. "He forgives them. He even forgives Jabez, I think. Letting these white birds go free is God's sign of forgiveness."

"You know a lot about gods," Argurios remarked.

She shrugged. "Not about Him. As I said, he's a strange god. I'm just making guesses."

The rain didn't cease, but a rainbow appeared over the rooftops of the city. The people stared at it in awe as they realized that it was a bridge that led them to Noah's ark waiting outside the city, below the end of the rainbow.

God had decided to spare his people.

"So, you used to be a priestess before you came here," Argurios said.

"Yes. A qadishtu, to be exact."

"A qadishtu?"

"A priestess who also serves as a sacred prostitute."

"Ah. Figures."

"And you used to be a warrior, back in Mycenae."

"Yes."

They watched in silence as the people of the city walked across the rainbow bridge to Noah's ark. Then, Arishat asked, "How do you like your new horse?"

Argurios grinned. "New horse? It's my good old friend Pegasus, except he's got wings now. I don't know. I must get used to this."

"You must get used to this? Be glad you don't have wings on your back. *That* takes getting used to."

They laughed. Just a day ago, they slept together on a dry bed, and now the city was flooded. They hovered above it with the help of angelic wings.

"Let's go somewhere we can get used to flying. Somewhere far away," Arishat suggested. "After everything that happened these last few days, I don't want to be anywhere near these people and their god anymore."

"Agreed. Where do you want to go? Egypt? Babylonia? Troy?" he asked.

"I don't care. There are many places in this world that I've never seen. It doesn't matter where we go so long as we go together. I love you, Argurios. Right now, all I want is to start a new life with you at my side."

"Sounds good. I always wanted to marry an angel," he said with a smirk.

They flew away into the sunset. It didn't matter where their path would take them. If the gods were merciful, they would send them somewhere peaceful, safe, and far away from the sea.

# BIOS

**Abad, Anne Carly** received the Poet of the Year Award in the 2017 Nick Joaquin Literary Awards. She has also been nominated for the Pushcart Prize and the Rhysling Award. Her work has appeared in *Apex*, *Mythic Delirium*, *Strange Horizons*, and many other publications. *We've Been Here Before*, her first poetry collection, is available through Aqueduct Press at http://www.aqueductpress.com/books/978-1-61976-222-0.php.

**Alexander, Terry** and his wife Phyllis live on a small farm near Porum, Oklahoma. They have three children, thirteen grandchildren, and eight great grandchildren. He has been published in various anthologies from Airship 27, OGHMA Creative Media, Pro Se Productions, and Pulp Cult. He is a member of the Tahlequah Writers, Oklahoma Writers Federation, Ozark Writers League, and Western Fictioneers.

**Ashley, Allen** is an award-winning writer, editor, and creative writing tutor based in London, UK. He is ex-president of the British Fantasy Society and the founder of the advanced science fiction and fantasy group Clockhouse London Writers. Published at over a hundred different venues, his most recent book is the poetry collection *Echoes from an Expired Earth* (Demain Publishing, UK, 2021), which was nominated for an Elgin Award. His next publication will be the chapbook *Journey to the Centre of the Onion* due from Eibonvale Press, UK in September 2023. Websites: www.allenashley.com and https://clockhouselondonwriters.wordpress.com/

**Bondoni, Gustavo** is a novelist and short story writer with over four hundred stories published in fifteen countries, in seven languages. He is a member of Codex and an active member of SFWA. He has published six science fiction novels including one trilogy, four monster books, a dark military fantasy, and a thriller. His short fiction is collected in *Pale Reflection* (2020), *Off the Beaten Path* (2019), *Tenth Orbit and Other Faraway Places* (2010) and *Virtuoso and Other Stories* (2011). In 2018, Bondoni received a Judges Commendation (and second place) in The James White Award. In 2019, he was awarded second place in the Jim Baen Memorial Contest. He was also a 2019 finalist in the Writers of the Future Contest. His website is at www.gustavobondoni.com.

**Conrad, Carl** lives in Grand Rapids, Michigan, and is a retired college economics instructor who enjoys writing of all types. He has published a children's fantasy novel, a biography of a Christian southern gospel singer, two imaginative sci-fi/action novels, and has written many short stories and essays.

**DeHart, JD** has been publishing for two decades. His work has appeared in *AIM*, *Modern Dad*, and *Steel Toe Review*. When he is not writing, he teaches English.

**Edwards (Dobbs), Kayleigh** is an author from South Wales who dwells happily amongst the free-roaming sheep and goats of the Welsh mountains. She is a writer of short fiction, plays, and non-fiction, all nestled somewhere between horror and comedy. She runs a horror review website called Happy Goat Horror (happygoathorror.com) that focuses on indie horror mostly, amongst other deliciously dastardly works. When she is not writing or reviewing books, she rants about games and movies on YouTube with her brother (Happy Goat Horror).

**Inverness, AmyBeth** is a historian and writer who takes inspiration from the realities and unknowns of humanity to write thought-provoking speculative fiction. She lives in the basement of a historic Denver mansion with her cat and a mostly harmless set of unidentifiable entities. You can find her stories in all the BLAS books and in the back of a desk drawer where they ferment like kombucha awaiting an audience with a suitable palate. Samples of both her millinery and fiction can be found at http://amybethinverness.com/.

**Johnson, Alex S.** is the author of several books, including *Bad Sunset*, *Wicked Candy*, and *Fucked Up Shit!* (co-authored with Berti Walker), and he is the creator of *Chunks: A Barfzaro Anthology*, *Floppy Shoes Apocalypse*, and the *Axes of Evil* heavy metal horror series. He lives in Sacramento, California.

**Macpherson, David** is a writer who lives in Central Massachusetts. His work has appeared in various anthologies and magazines.

**Mollica, Tom** lives in West Milwaukee, Wisconsin and is the owner of Studio Tommy – a digital media company.

**Pauff, H.L.** is a writer living in Baltimore who spends his nights mashing on keyboard and looking for the magic to happen.

**Sawielijew, Frank** has the blood of Russian nobility in his veins and the most beautiful woman in the world at his side. He lives near the city of Frankfurt, Germany, where he works as a historian. When he isn't busy trying to unveil the secrets of the past, he likes to create fantastic worlds of his own. In this, he draws inspiration from a variety of sources ranging from old Babylonian cuneiform texts to classic 1990s PC games. He writes short stories and novels in both English and German. *Die Kleine Gelbe Kröte*, his first novel, was published in 2013.

**Stephens, Lorina** has worked as an editor and a freelance journalist for national and regional print media; she is the author of seven books, both fiction and non-fiction; she's been a festival organizer, and a publicist; she lectures on many topics from historical textiles and domestic technologies to publishing and writing; she teaches; and she continues to work as a writer, artist, and publisher at Five Rivers Publishing. She has had several short fiction pieces published in Canada's acclaimed *On Spec* magazine, *Postscripts to Darkness, Neo-Opsis, Garden of Eden*, and Marion Zimmer Bradley's fantasy anthology *Sword & Sorceress X.* **Vernetti, Sarah** lives in Las Vegas. When she isn't writing about travel, she's crafting short stories and flash fiction. In what feels like a former life, she earned a master's degree in art history. Follow her on Twitter: @SarahVernetti.

**Vicary, John** began publishing poetry in the fifth grade and has been writing ever since. A contributor to many compendiums, his most recent credentials include short fiction in the collections *The Longest Hours, Midnight Circus, Something's Brewing*, and *Temporary Skeletons*. He has stories in upcoming issues of *Disturbed Digest* and *Dead Men's Tales*. He enjoys playing piano and lives in rural Michigan with his family. You can read more of his work at keppiehed.com.

**Wynn, E.S.** is the author of over seventy books and the chief editor at Thunderune Publishing. In his spare time, he spins stories, builds board games, stitches together battle jackets, runs a pair of magazines, makes videos about Norse Shamanism on YouTube, and encourages people to create new art. He is openly transgender and seeks to establish acceptance and love for and within the trans community. He has worked with hundreds of authors and edited thousands of manuscripts for nearly a dozen different magazines. His stories and articles have been published in dozens of journals, e-zines, and anthologies. He has taught classes in literature, marketing, math, spirituality, energetic healing, and guided meditation, and he has worked as a voice-over artist for several horror and sci-fi podcasts, albums, and e-books.

# ABOUT THE EDITOR

**Allen Taylor** is the publisher at Garden Gnome Publications and editor of the Biblical Legends Antology Series. His fiction and poetry have been published online and in print. He is the author of two non-fiction books on the intersection between cryptocurrency and social media as well as a spiritual testimony titled *I Am Not the King*, all available at Amazon. He is the creator of the #twitpoem hashtag at Twitter and writes a newsletter/blog at Paragraph. He is a freelance writer and book editor at Taylored Content.

If you liked *Deluge: Stories of Survival & Tragedy in the Great Flood*, the editor and the authors would sincerely invite you to write a review at Amazon, Goodreads, or wherever you purchased this book.

And we thank you from the bottom of our hearts, as do the garden gnomes.

Also look at *Garden of Eden*, the first book in the Biblical Legends Anthology Series, and *Sulfurings: Tales from Sodom & Gomorrah*.

Please report errors in this e-book to the editor at editor@gardengnomepubs.com.

# Connect With the Gnomes

The garden gnomes would sincerely like to connect with you at our social media outposts. Please, drop on by!

Follow our editor on Twitter, Hive, and Paragraph.

# Books By Allen Taylor

## Garden of Eden

The first book in the Biblical Legends Anthology Series, *Garden of Eden* is a multi-author anthology that explores themes related to the creation story. Not Christian but not anti-Christian.

**An excerpt from a reader review:**

> To answer the obvious question first, while some of the contributors might be Christian, this is not a Christian book; nor is it an attack on Christianity. The works, some more than others, do raise issues of morality and sin, but they are neither thinly veiled allegory nor brutal parody.

## Sulfurings: Tales from Sodom & Gomorrah

The second book in the Biblical Legends Anthology Series, *Sulfurings: Tales from Sodom & Gomorrah* is more horrific and apocalyptic than *Garden of Eden*. It also includes more stories from a more diverse group of authors.

**From a reader review:**

> While *Garden of Eden* was almost lighthearted in its biblical fiction, *Sulfurings* was much darker, and gritty. The details of the horrors were almost palatable. At times, I imagined I could smell the sulfur and feel the terror of those of Sodom. I almost felt sorry for them, almost.

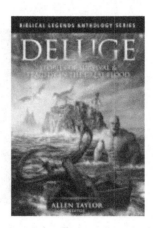

## Deluge: Stories of Survival & Tragedy in the Great Flood

The third book in the Biblical Legends Anthology Series. *Deluge: Stories of Survival & Tragedy in the Great Flood* takes a weirder turn than the *Garden of Eden* and *Sulfurings*, but the quality of the writing is superb. It also seems to be an audience favorite.

**Check out this excerpt from a reader review:**

> I have a lot of respect for the work of the editor of this multi-author volume of deluge-related stories. Mr. Taylor has gone to a lot of work to put it together. All the stories and poetic prose in this book are excellent
> work.

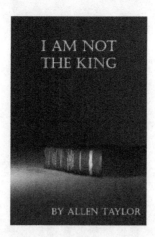

## I Am Not the King

*I Am Not the King* is Allen Taylor's Christian testimony. Beginning with childhood, he details the events while growing up in a legalistic Holiness environment with a father dealing with angry issues and how that impacted his life as a young man. With a stunning twist, he tells how an atheist college professor drove him back to Jesus and what living as a Christian for thirty years has taught him about forgiveness and grace.

**An excerpt from a reader review:**

> Allen's recognition of the miseries and worldly woes and wrongdoing is the starting point for his search for his real life. This is the story of his search and rescue history. His scathing descriptions of family members, his parents and others, paint large an in-your-face, no-holds-barred, no-punches-pulled, full-frontal exposure of what it's like to be lost with no guidance in the worldly world, always searching for something, something to grasp hold of and hold onto, something solid, something worthy of his trust.

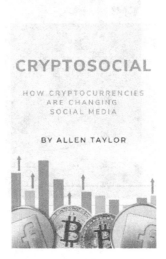

## Cryptosocial: How Cryptocurrencies Are Changing Social Media

Written for a general audience, *Cryptosocial: How Cryptocurrencies Are Changing Social Media* details the history of the World Wide Web to illustrate its decentralized beginnings and helps readers understand the basics of blockchain technology and cryptocurrencies. With that understanding, he goes on to detail the growing number of social media platforms where participants can earn cryptocurrencies for their postings.

**An excerpt from a reader review:**

> While the reality of a decentralized social media is the hope of many people who are concerned—or fed up—with the unchecked clout and excessive influence of legacy media and behemoths like Facebook, Google, and Twitter, the path to decentralization won't be easy. Even so, the book strikes a balance between caution and optimism.

## Web3 Social: How Creators Are Changing the World Wide Web

## (And You Can Too!)

*Web3 Social: How Creators Are Changing the World Wide Web (And You Can Too!)* is written for the creator class to illustrate how the creator economy is expanding with new monetization protocols, the ability to protect intellectual property and digital identities using blockchain tools, and how creators are going direct to their fans by building their own platforms with Web3 tools of decentralization.

**From a reader review:**

> As someone who is a four-time self-published author right here on Amazon, and who is old enough now to look back at years on both centralized and decentralized social media and compare, the rightness of this book is perfectly apparent to me. I simply do not want to have my creative life controlled by people who see me only as a chattel. Mr. Taylor shows us creatives the way out of that entrapment.

Made in the USA
Monee, IL
27 March 2024

55231656R00085